BEST LAID PLANS

DARA GIRARD

ILORI
Press Books, LLC

ISBN: 978-1949764505

BEST LAID PLANS

Published by ILORI Press Books

ILORI PRESS BOOKS, LLC

P.O. Box 10332

Silver Spring, MD 20914

www.iloripressbooks.com

BOOKS BY DARA GIRARD

Duvall Sisters

The Glass Slipper Project

Taming Mariella

A Reluctant Hero

The Black Stockings Society

Power Play

A Gentleman's Offer

Body Chemistry

Round the Clock

Return of the Black Stockings Society

Playing for Keeps

After Hours

A Private Affair

Just One Look

Private Lessons

The Main Attraction

Ladies of the Pen

Words of Seduction

Pages of Passion

Beneath the Covers

Henson Series

Table for Two

Gaining Interest

Careless Rapture

Dangerous Curves

Familiar Stranger

It Happened One Wedding

Unexpected Pleasure

Midnight Promise

Sweet Temptation

Always and Forever

Truly Yours

Say Yes

Picture Perfect

Clifton Sisters

The Sapphire Pendant

The Amber Stone

The Emerald Ring

Fortune Brothers

A Tempting Proposal

A Seductive Arrangement

An Unforgettable Moment

Novels

Honest Betrayal

The Daughters of Winston Barnett

Remember My Name

Illusive Flame

Winterwood Lane

Promise Me

This Changes Everything

Sparks

Piece of Cake

Someone was trying to kill him. That was the only explanation Damon Reemer could come up with for the loud buzzer that threatened to make his head explode.

"Do you want me to answer that?" a soft feminine voice asked next to him.

He made a grunting noise. It was all he could manage at the time. Everything about his body ached and he'd do anything to make the noise stop. He felt the bed shift as his companion left and soon silence followed. Beautiful, sweet silence. He sighed ready to drift back to sleep.

"Damon? Damon! It's time to wake up!"

Damon groaned and tried to slide deeper under the covers. The voice wasn't soft and feminine—it was loud and masculine and seemed determined to bust his eardrums.

"Damon did you hear me?"

"People in Australia could hear you," Damon grumbled.

"Then get up."

"Give him some time," the feminine voice said. He felt her

warm lips on his cheek then she whispered, "You were wonderful. Call me," and then she was gone.

"Are you ready to wake up now?" the male voice demanded.

No, he could sleep forever, but he knew that wouldn't happen. Damon slowly opened his eyes as though it were a monumental effort. The way his head felt the effort alone was a big achievement to focus his gaze on the room he was in. He glanced around trying to orient himself and figure out where he was. Because he traveled the world as a celebrity chef, it wasn't unusual for him to wake up in a hotel bedroom (or someone else's) and not remember how he'd gotten there.

His gaze fell on a framed mosaic painting on the wall in front of him then drifted to the large picture window over to the side that gave him a view of the trees outside. One tree loomed large, its leaves unchanged to signify the presence of autumn. How he hated that damn tree. The tree wasn't an evergreen and its leaves were supposed to be turning yellow or brown and dying. Instead they were still bright green and looked as though they were ready for spring, but thankfully he knew he was home.

He removed his gaze from the window and let it land on the tall figure standing in front of his bed. The figure was too filled with indignation to be his house manager, Ray so he guessed it had to be his brother. He inwardly sighed.

He didn't want to see him, but at least his brother looked like it was the middle of October. He wore a thick, deep red, hand knit sweater, dark blue jeans and a determined expression Damon knew only too well. He closed his eyes. "Give me another hour," he said.

"Come on, it's nearly one o'clock," Leo said glancing impatiently at his watch.

"So what?"

"It's time to start the day. Who was that woman who just left?"

Damon frowned trying to get through the brain fog. He had no idea. "What did she look like?" he asked, hoping to jog his memory.

"Long legs, killer smile, gorgeous. But that's nothing new for you."

"Hmm."

"Bet you don't even know her name," his brother said with a smirk. "But she looked familiar."

Damon lifted himself up on his elbow and glanced at the clock on his bedside table. "What do you want?"

Leo ignored the question. "But that doesn't narrow the list. She could be a model or an actress or a dancer or a—"

Damon made his voice stronger. "What are you doing here?"

"Making sure you're still alive."

Damon stiffened startled by his brother's choice of words. "What do you mean by that?"

"You got us all worried. You cancelled a major function then disappeared for nearly a week. No email, no text, no phone. Nothing. We didn't have any way to get a hold of you. If I hadn't found you here today I was going to call the cops."

"You're my brother—"

"And manager," Leo added.

"Yes and manager, but you're not my babysitter. You know I can take care of myself and I like to disappear sometimes."

"Not like this. Usually at least *someone* knows where you are. Did anything happen? Is something wrong?"

Yes, something had happened. And something was very wrong. Something so big it had changed his life. Forever. For a moment Damon's mind cleared and he remembered the doctor visits and the dire diagnosis and his desperate desire to escape it all. Damon opened his mouth to share then stopped. He wasn't ready to tell anyone. Not yet. "No, nothing's wrong."

Leo studied him clearly doubtful, but he didn't pursue the topic. When he didn't say anything, Damon said, "Why else are you here?"

"You have a hangover," his brother said flatly then sat down on the light colored recliner off to the side.

Damon rubbed his temples in no mood to argue the obvious. "That wasn't my question."

Leo's gaze grew more intense. "You don't drink. You haven't had a hangover in years. You like to be in control of every situation. The last time you got plastered was when Granddad died."

Damon briefly closed his eyes remembering "Popa" the affectionate name he used to call his granddad as a child; the man who had been his rock and champion. He'd guided and believed in him when few others did. Damon had spent hours in the kitchen watching and learning how to cook with his grandfather when he traveled to Jamaica for his summer holidays. He'd make Damon his thick and creamy oats porridge served with chopped pears, a dish that Damon considered a cherished staple of his childhood. Popa had a large piece of property and in addition to showing Damon how to plant and grow a variety of vegetables, he shared with him the spices and herbs he skillfully used to transform any dish into an edible delight. Popa also took him around the island to experience different cultures and they would go on excursions to Indian, Chinese and German restaurants.

He died just when Damon had started to become known. It had crushed him and he'd tried to bury his sorrows with rum, just as he had last night. "Guess I'll be seeing you soon, Popa," he mumbled.

"What?"

Damon looked up at his brother. "Nothing, I just got a little carried away," he said.

Leo's frown increased. "But you never—"

Damon's patience snapped. "What do you want, Leo? Get to the point or leave."

Leo sighed fiercely. "It's about that Apprentice Program of yours."

"What about it?"

"I think you should close it."

"No." Damon slid back under the covers and pulled them over his head. "Goodbye."

Leo yanked the sheets away. "We have to talk about this."

Damon glared up at him. "There's nothing to talk about. I'm not shutting it down."

"You have to. It's losing money."

"I don't care."

"You should care!"

Damon covered his ears. "Do you have to shout?"

Leo lowered his voice and returned to his seat. "I didn't shout, but I will if that is what it will take for you to hear me."

"I hear you, but I'm not closing it."

"It will bleed you dry." His brother folded his arms. "Shut it down. Bury it and put it to rest."

Damon stared at Leo then glanced away. It wasn't the first time his brother had made that suggestion. The Apprenticeship Program, for out-of-work individuals, meant a lot to him. It offered people a chance to get paid to learn a new skill and then get back into the job market. He'd partnered with two homeless shelters and a local non-profit organization that worked with out-of-work individuals and heard that it had been extremely beneficial getting people back to work and lifting their morale.

Unfortunately, with his busy travel schedule, he hadn't been able to get to all his commitments and hadn't been diligent in overseeing the program although he had a small office on the premises. After the first year, he had left ninety-nine percent of its operation to the director. It had been five months since Damon's last visit inside the two-story, white brick building in downtown Oak Lawn, Maryland. A city with a minor identity crisis.

Status conscious residents referred to it as a DC suburb, less concerned residents called it Okay and those outside of the place rarely called it anything at all. But business prospectors always saw Oak Lawn as an opportunity. It had great untapped real estate and a class of people with disposable income.

Luckily with Damon's family connections and money, he'd had no difficulty buying the prime piece of real estate, which was conveniently located on a bus line making it accessible for both the students of the culinary program and the general public.

But despite the building's beauty and the pride he had in his project, he hadn't been able to give the program the focus it needed. He'd been more tired lately—lethargic. For a man known for his exuberance and excessive energy it was a major blow and starting to affect his work. Twice he'd had to cancel engagements and nearly passed out at a cooking demonstration. It was one of the reasons he'd decided to disappear for a week.

It was his heart the doctors said and something to do with his blood. There was nothing they could do and they encouraged him to take things easy. But he didn't care. He wasn't going to sit around and wait to die and he wasn't going to give up on his program. Most thought he'd named it after himself, but he'd named it for his grandfather whose name he shared.

"It's helping people," he said.

Leo leaped out his seat and threw up his hand exasperated. "It's a damn charity. If you want to help people, donate blood, give money, pay a kid's tuition in Africa or Asia, but this idea makes no business sense. You're wasting valuable resources."

"I'm not wasting anything."

"You can help from a safe, sensible distance."

That was what his family did. They were always a step away from a problem. They donated to key causes. His mother headed a couple fundraisers and his father sat on several boards for large corporations, but Damon had wanted to do something different because of Angela. *Angela.* He hadn't seen her in two years and just the thought of her name filled him with pain and regret. She'd assumed he was superficial and selfish and he'd wanted to prove her wrong.

He'd started the Damon Reemer Culinary Apprenticeship Program (also known as DRCA) six years ago while working with Angela, hoping she would see him for who he was. But after working together for four years they had parted ways when she'd thought he'd betrayed her and she had never forgiven him. She'd ignored his repeated phone calls and emails, and refused to see him when he twice stopped by her office, never giving him a chance to explain. He hadn't seen her in two years.

He quickly pushed the memory of her aside. But what had started out as a project to ease his wounded ego and help him deal with the grief of his Popa's death had become important and dear to him. He'd worked hard to make sure it would be successful and had talked to key advisors in the food industry and hired a top-notch chef. But in spite of all his efforts the program couldn't sustain itself and every year he was forced to spend more money to keep it running. It seemed his vision was headed for failure and he rarely failed.

But he wouldn't give up. If it was the last thing he did, he would not close the program.

Damon rested back against the headboard and kept his voice firm. "I said no."

"The restaurant industry isn't what it used to be. In this recession there aren't as many places to employ graduates. You're giving people skills they can't use and paying them to learn. It just doesn't make good business sense." His brother shoved his hands in his pockets as he paced the room.

He could feel his brother's frustration and fear. The restaurant industry was hurting. Fine dining had given way to fast food chains as people tried to stretch their budgets. The recession had gripped the world in an ugly stranglehold and although a new administration with a fresh faced former senator offering change and hope was now at the helm, many things felt uncertain.

The early 2000s seemed to be littered with uncertainty. The 2001 September 11 terrorist attack had shaken the beginning of the decade and it seemed the decade wouldn't end on a high note either.

But one thing Damon knew was at a time when people were losing homes, jobs and worse of all hope, he needed to provide a solution. He needed to offer a chance to train or retain people with skills they could use in the future. The industry would rebound as well as other food focused businesses.

Unfortunately, he wasn't sure his program would last

much longer without some help. But giving up wasn't something he liked to contemplate. He sent his brother a steady glare.

"Leo."

His brother stopped pacing and looked at him. "What?"

"This discussion is over." Which meant they were never to discuss it again.

CHAPTER TWO

*L*eo let his shoulders droop knowing he couldn't fight his brother anymore. He looked around the room then picked up a bright pink bra from the nightstand. "She left this."

"Who's she?" Damon asked trying to follow the conversation.

"The mystery woman who left." Leo frowned. "You must have really partied hard to forget a woman so quickly. That's not like you. You're usually good with names." He suddenly snapped his fingers as a thought came to him. "Channel Eight."

Damon squinted at him, annoyed by the snapping sound. "What?"

"I remember where I've seen her. She's the anchorwoman on Channel Eight!"

"And you got that from looking at her bra?"

"It jogged my memory because...uh...never mind."

Damon sniffed amused. He would have laughed if he didn't know his head would hurt. His older brother was a lot shyer and more timid when it came to women. He was Damon's complete opposite. Damon loved women. All women. Young, old, fat, slim. He loved their company and their looks and the many pleasures they offered him. He'd spent most of his life enjoying them and didn't plan to stop.

"Anyway," Leo said carefully folding the bra as though it might jump up and bite him. He placed it aside. "You're not yourself."

Damon pushed the sheets aside and swung his feet over the side of the bed. It didn't appear as if his brother would leave him alone anytime soon. "Hmm."

"Or maybe this is a sign."

"A sign?"

"Yes, that you should settle down."

Damon paused and narrowed his eyes, a trickle of unease coursing through him. "You just sounded like mother."

A look of guilt flashed across Leo's face. "That's because she's coming by this afternoon."

Damon swore and jumped to his feet then quickly regretted the decision when the world started to spin. He fell back down on the bed and held his head in his hands. He swore again.

"It's not that bad," Leo said surprised by his brother's coarse language. Damon glared at him and Leo cleared his throat. "I mean it doesn't have to be," he corrected.

"Why didn't you tell me she was coming in the first place?"

"I didn't want to wake you up with that kind of news. At least I'm here to warn you."

He stood. "How much time do I have?"

"Three hours."

"Good. Tell her I had a meeting."

Leo took out his electronic organizer. "But you don't."

"Make it up."

"You're not going to disappear again."

"Why not?"

"You have to see her."

Damon sighed. Leo was right. He'd have to see his mother eventually. He couldn't disappear forever. "What does she want?"

"She's worried about you."

"What is there to worry about? I'm rich, successful—"

"And single," Leo finished with a smug grin.

Damon shrugged then grabbed his robe from the back of his door. "You make it sound like a disease."

"To her it is."

He tied the sash of his robe then left his bedroom and headed downstairs to the kitchen. He didn't need something to eat, but definitely something to drink. His mouth felt like he'd swallowed cotton. "Then why doesn't she bother you?"

Leo followed him. "I'm engaged, remember?"

Damon snorted unimpressed. He opened the fridge and saw it. His hangover cocktail. He loved his housekeeper and made a mental note to give her a raise. She must have seen him when he got home. She had been there following his grandfather's funeral, and knowing that Damon wasn't a heavy drinker and seeing the state he was in, had graciously offered to make him "something" she used to make for her father, to help him recover from a night of drinking.

Damon ripped off the cling film covering the glass and took a long swallow then set the glass down.

"You think my engagement is funny?" Leo asked.

"You've been engaged for four years." Damon responded, a note of distain in his voice.

Leo tapped the side of his nose. "That's because I'm a smart man."

"Or Joyce is a dumb woman," Damon mumbled.

"I heard that."

"How can you keep it up? She's going to want to set a date one day."

Leo shrugged unconcerned. "She lives on hope. If you were smart like me you'd do the same." He sat on one of the swivel chairs at the kitchen island.

Damon leaned against the counter. "Con a woman into an engagement so I can make my mother happy?"

Leo frowned. "It's not like that. I'm going to marry her."

"When?"

"Eventually," he said annoyed. "But we're not talking about me. I know that something's up. When's the last time you shaved?"

Damon touched the stubble on his chin. If he wasn't careful in a few days he'd have a beard. "I don't know."

"Listen to me. Find a nice woman and get engaged. I have to admit I'm worried about you too. Why did you refuse the European Cuisine Show?"

"I didn't feel in the mood."

"You'd get to go to Italy."

"I've been there before." And Paris and Moscow and South Africa and a number of other places. Damon was one of the best chefs in the world known for his exotic, ethnic dishes that fused Caribbean and Indian cuisine. He had cooked for princes and kings, governors and diplomats, been on television, in magazines, and had three bestsellers. At one point, last year, he even made a cameo in a blockbuster film. He'd dated beautiful women, skied in Aspen and surfed in Tahiti. He lived a life most people would envy and never had it all felt so hollow. "I just wasn't interested."

Leo looked at him stunned. "Not interested?"

"Yes," he said knowing he wouldn't be able to explain why.

"You're just tired. I knew you wouldn't be able to keep up this lifestyle of yours."

"Is there an 'I told you so' somewhere?" His brother was always telling him to slow down, which was also one of their differences. Aside from women, Damon was impulsive where Leo was methodical; he loved to take risks, while Leo liked to be safe. But Leo and his sister, Helen, were just like their parents. Not only had Leo inherited their more cautious nature, he'd gotten their light brown eyes, fine features and toffee colored skin. Damon knew he was the black sheep of the family in more ways than one. Aside from his temperament he was dark—from his eyes, which could turn onyx when he was angry, to the color of his skin.

Leo frowned, hearing the sarcasm in his brother's voice. "It's much better than the schedule you're keeping up. Why don't you admit that the DRCA Program is a giant noose and let it go?"

"No."

Leo shook his head. "All this is going to wear you down. You're thirty-six, you know. You're not going to live forever."

Damon sighed and placed his glass in the sink no longer able to look at his brother. "I know that better than you think."

CHAPTER THREE

"You don't belong here."

It wasn't the first time Angela Watkins had heard those words in her thirty-four years. The first time was at a friend's thirteenth birthday party when another girl laughed at her hand-me-down clothes and told her that she must have gotten lost. Then at college when she tried to pledge a sorority, then at her first job where she was one of only five women in a team of twenty. But she hadn't expected to hear those words now at the Damon Reemer Culinary Apprenticeship Program. It was her only source of income and the best chance to get her life back on track. She was desperate to save enough money to get out of her friend's cramped basement before her baby was born.

Angela looked at her instructor, Ricardo Denson, a wiry man in his late fifties with dyed black hair. "I'm doing my best," she said in a calm voice.

Her tone seemed to aggravate him more. He looked at her work station where her attempt at making a soufflé was a complete disaster. "Your best is the worse I've ever seen." Ricardo spun around and raised his hand as well as his voice. "Class, let me give you a perfect example of what not to do." He then went down a list of all the things she'd done wrong, from the way she'd organized her tools to the oil she'd used in her recipe. "That's enough class continue with what you were doing." He lowered his voice and looked at Angela. "You don't have what it takes."

"I'm just a little awkward."

Ricardo looked down at her protruding belly with undisguised disgust. "Is that what you call it?"

Angela knew she hadn't been able to keep up with the other students. The only reason she was still in the program was at the insistence of its director, Serena Logan, who she'd know from the past. Angela had met her years ago when she had worked with Damon Reemer.

After her life started to go into a free fall, Angela had reached out to Serena hoping to do some freelance work for her, but Serena didn't have anything. However, when Angela shared how dire her situation was, Serena offered her space in her basement and reminded her about the apprenticeship program.

Angela had resisted at first. She didn't want anything to do with the shallow, arrogant Damon Reemer, but when Serena told her how much she felt it could benefit her and that Damon rarely, if ever, bothered visiting (thus reducing the risk that she'd ever see him) Angela knew she couldn't refuse the offer. She knew from working with him that Damon always let other people run things for him. She clearly remembered that when he first started the Apprentice Program he only made three appearances that year, leaving Serena in charge of everything.

However, Serena's assurance did little to quiet Angela's fears. During the first week, Angela entered the building with trepidation and kept looking around in case she saw him. Thankfully, she never did and started to relax. But her relaxation soon turned into panic when she realized one major thing—she couldn't cook.

She tried her hardest but failed every time. She couldn't catch on how to crack open an egg without bits of the shell falling into the bowl or how to heat oil without burning it. Each time she failed Ricardo would complain and threaten to fire her, but Serena helped smooth things over with him, knowing how much Angela needed the money and the health insurance.

However, time and luck seemed to be running out. She worked hard in spite of the setbacks created by fatigue, backaches and her ever growing belly. When she'd started the program she was only six months along and could move faster. Now every movement seemed slow and graceless. As her pregnancy progressed there were things she couldn't do such as reach certain shelves and equipment. But despite the struggle Angela was determined to keep up, ignoring the times when her legs throbbed, her ankles swelled and her back muscle constricted or when she felt like locking herself in the freezer because she felt overheated.

Angela knew she had no choice. She had to push through all the discomfort if she was going to be able to take care of the child growing inside her.

She was going to have a boy. The thought of him eased some of her sadness. She couldn't wait to hold her son in her arms, to count his fingers and toes and stroke his cheek and look into his eyes...

Ricardo's voice cut through her thoughts. "Ms. Watkins, did you hear what I said?"

"I will improve," she promised.

"Not in *my* class." He turned and walked away before she could argue.

Angela opened her mouth then closed it in defeat. She'd been humiliated enough and now she just wanted to leave. She reached back to untie her apron but could barely reach the knot. Not only was she awkward, she was aware of her appearance. Her white shirt had become too tight and she'd stained her black maternity trousers, but buying new clothes was not a priority. She needed to save every penny so that she could rent an apartment and buy things for the baby. Thankfully, once she finished the program and was placed in a job, Serena had told her she knew of a woman who could look after the baby while Angela worked since the precarious state of her life didn't give Angela the choice of maternity leave.

She only had four weeks left to her due date and she felt like an elephant. And now she felt like a failure. At last she undid the knot and yanked the string. Her elbow hit a plastic pitcher. It fell to the floor, thankfully empty, but the sound of it bouncing before it settled on the ground echoed through the large kitchen. She began to reach for it when Ricardo said in a curt tone, "Leave it." He made an expressive gesture towards the door. "Just go."

Angela looked around at the other students seeing their looks of pity. She dropped her apron on the counter, grabbed her purse off a hook nearby then left.

She shut the door behind her then lumbered down the hallway fighting back tears. Where would she be able to find a job? A stray tear escaped down her cheek and she angrily brushed it aside. How could her life have turned out like this? Only a year ago she'd been a successful marketing specialist at an advertising company then the recession hit and she'd lost all of her investments when the business went bankrupt. But she hadn't been worried; she was in a solid relationship with her fiancé, Ronald Tidewater. They'd been together for seven years, five of them engaged (the long engagement was so they could focus on their careers—or so he told her). He said he didn't mind supporting her while she freelanced and did some consulting. Then she got pregnant.

A complete surprise and not part of the plan.

She later learned that a new herbal remedy she'd used to treat mild depression and sleep issues had interfered with the effectiveness of her birth control pills. Fortunately, she and Ronald had planned on kids. He'd been happy at first then three months into her pregnancy he said he wasn't ready and left.

As the recession took hold, her client list slowly dried up. She lived on her savings hoping for something to work out. Nothing did.

In a matter of months Angela discovered how empty her life had been. All her high flying friends had disappeared along with her fiancé and his biweekly salary. She had no one to turn to. Her mother, Ms. Elma Mae Watkins, lived in a senior retirement community in Lynwood, in a neighboring county that boasted fewer residents and a lower cost of living, and with her fragile health, Angela feared her mother wouldn't be able to handle what was happening to her daughter. Her mother was a proud woman and would not approve of a daughter of hers disgracing the family name. Her mother expected her life to be better than hers. "You must make my struggle worth it," she constantly reminded her. "I do this all for you." Her mother would see Angela's life as a shame and would never understand how a college educated daughter of hers could be out of work and with no place of her own since Ronald's name was the only one on the house deed, which he used to sell the house from under her.

Unfortunately, Angela didn't know where her father was and she and her sister had a complicated relationship.

"You should give the baby up for adoption," Megan said as she and Angela sat on her sister's wraparound porch with blue trim and beveled glass windows and door. Megan lived well and had worked for every cent as one of the youngest information system managers at her company.

Her sister was an attractive woman with thick eyebrows and dark brown eyes. She was slender in a way Angela sometimes envied, with straight black hair that fell to her shoulders. She wore understated jewelry, which was usually gold to compliment the yellow undertone of her honey brown skin.

Angela blinked at first not understanding and doubting what her sister was saying. "What?"

"You heard me the first time."

"But why?"

"Simple economics, you can't afford a baby."

"I can with the right job."

"Which you don't have right now. I can't believe—" She stopped and looked away.

"You can't believe what?" Angela pressed.

Megan made an impatient motion with her shoulders. "I can't believe I have to explain this to you."

"Try," Angela said through clenched teeth.

"You know how hard it was to grow up with a single parent. I can't believe you'd do that to your own kid."

"But things will work out. I'm not Mom. I have a graduate degree and marketable skills. I'll get back on my feet again soon," Angela said, wishing she knew when that would be.

Megan reached for her purse and pulled out her checkbook. "How much do you need?"

Angela stared at her sister for a long moment realizing how different they were. When they were younger they used to be closer, now they were more like strangers. She'd come to her sister for comfort and emotional support not as a charity. That's when she knew her plan to stay with her wouldn't work.

"I don't need anything," she said knowing it was a lie, but her pride wouldn't let her retract.

Megan shook her head. "Yes, you do. Don't be stubborn." She scribbled an amount down then ripped the cheque out of her chequebook and held it out to her. "Please think about what I said." When Angela ignored the cheque, she let her hand fall to her lap. "It's not really that hard a decision, is it? Ronald was a bastard. I knew it every time he would put off setting a date to marry you."

"We were busy," Angela said as a feeble defense.

"Mom worked so hard for us to have a better life than she did, if she knew what was going on with you and how Ronald—"

Angela stiffened. "Don't you say a word to her."

Megan brushed her sister's fears aside. "I wouldn't dare, but I want you to really consider what you're doing. How much is at stake. I know there's a couple out there who would love to raise this kid."

Angela ignored the cheque. "You mean *my* kid."

"I love you, Angela, and I want what's best for you. I know all of this is overwhelming." Megan reached over and covered

Angela's hand. "Let me handle this for you. I've carefully thought it through and I believe it's the best option."

Angela snatched her hand away, hating how her sister spoke to her as though she were a wayward child. She stood. "I can take care of myself. Goodbye."

"You're making a mistake," Megan called after her. "Give yourself time to think things through."

Angela stormed to her Mercedes SUV, one thing Ronald hadn't managed to take from her. "I have."

"You're being angry at the wrong person. Ronald's the jerk not me. You know that I love you and I only want what's best for you."

Angela opened her car door.

"If you won't take my advice, at least take my money," she heard Megan say before she slammed the car door shut.

Angela left that day and hadn't spoken to her sister since. Now she had no family to turn to. Angela leaned against a wall, taking in deep breaths. How could she have worked so hard, planned so long only to end up as her mother had—a single mother with few options? Although she was grateful to Serena for the basement room, she'd dreamed of having her own apartment. And the one thing she wanted most was to rent a two bedroom place and create a nursery before the holidays. Without a job that dream was impossible. Angela felt defeated. For a moment she thought of her mother's early experience when she came to the US. She was pregnant with Megan and the only living space she could find for herself and Angela was a damp, dark basement. Eventually a large suitcase doubled as Megan's crib when she was born. Angela shuddered at the prospect that her son would face a similar predicament.

Twice she'd thought about giving up her baby, but just as quickly dismissed the idea. She wanted this child and didn't want to have to explain why. But part of her felt selfish because she knew how hard life would be. She knew there were many single mothers who were pleased with their choice and children who were or had been happy growing up in a single parent home, but it hadn't been so for her or her sister.

Although they loved their mother, an immigrant from Barbados, who did her best to provide for them, it wasn't always enough. Her mother was usually tired, sad or both.

But she knew her mother hadn't always been that way. Elma Mae had been a vivacious young woman who'd had a whirlwind romance with a charming vacationer, whom she'd quickly married. She soon gave him a daughter and accepted his frequent absences from the tiny house they shared with her parents, a grandmother and brother. He told her he traveled for business and she believed him when he sent her to come to America, which had been her first time on an airplane.

But when he promptly abandoned her, their four year old daughter and unborn child for another family she'd never known about, Elma Mae's youthful joy faded away to bitterness and determination. She wouldn't return in shame to her parents' house. She'd make it on her own.

Angela had no memory of her father—her mother had destroyed every picture of him—and refused to name him.

Angela remembered a childhood of struggle and survival. Most of her school days, from elementary through middle school, had been spent coming home straight after school and heating up leftovers or frozen dinners about to expire from some weekly store sale, cleaning the house and when she was older, getting a job after school to help pay the rent and looking after her little sister. Her mother didn't have a family to help them and Angela never knew who or where their father was. The one great fortune was that their local public schools were part of a magnet program initiative that offered quality education for free, giving them an academic advantage other lower income districts didn't have.

However, that didn't stop Angela from envying her friends who had both parents and she sometimes resented the life her mother had created for them.

"But this time will be different," she whispered touching her stomach. She pushed herself from the wall and continued walking aimlessly down the hall. She could go up to Serena's office, but she didn't feel like talking right now. She had to come up with another plan.

She stopped when she saw a huge black and white photo of Damon Reemer and his latest bestselling cookbook, prominently displayed on an easel at the entrance to The Spicy Papaya Restaurant. The restaurant was connected to the school and provided 'on the job' training for graduates of the program. It was a contemporary facility that offered world class cuisine for adventurous patrons who could afford it.

He was gorgeous, rich and charming. Even in black and white his engaging smile and dark eyes were magnetic and she knew in real life he was even more devastating. No photograph could capture his sinfully rich cocoa skin and roguish good looks. She'd met him over six years ago when he was a minor celebrity chef with a new restaurant and fifteen minutes of fame that she knew could extend into an empire.

Eager to build her client list, she'd contacted him after seeing him take third place in a nationally televised cooking competition. She knew the winner and runner-up would be hounded with offers, but Angela saw a goldmine in the intense chef who'd gotten the nickname 'Demon Damon' because the hotter the stakes the better he got and whenever someone had to compete against him they broke out in a sweat. Unfortunately, he was finally defeated by two contestants whose styles were more amenable to the judges and TV audience.

But she felt she'd won the prize when he'd said yes to her offer.

She knew the smile he flashed in his publicity photo had been hard won. He was a man who didn't smile or laugh easily. It was something she'd had to coax out of him. In the past he'd been too intense and driven to be charming, but she'd managed to draw that trait out of him and while he wasn't a natural, he was a quick study and soon was charming everyone he met.

But aside from his apparent attributes—intelligent, driven—she'd soon discovered that he was arrogant, stubborn, spoiled and a danger to most women who didn't know better than to avoid him. Fortunately, she hadn't fallen into that category.

She had been recently hired at McClintok, a PR firm in downtown DC, and he had been her first big client. She wanted to prove to her boss that she had good instincts on choosing a local man, who some dismissed as a rich kid dabbling in an expensive hobby. Damon used Reemer, the surname of her maternal grandfather, to separate himself from the more known Branson name he'd been born with.

She'd succeeded. By the time she was finished with a campaign that not only heightened the visibility for his flag-ship restaurant but expanded his brand, Damon Reemer wasn't only known in the US but also overseas. She'd even made sure that his first book hit the bestseller's list by working closely with his publisher's in-house publicist, and had gotten him featured on the Food Network more than once after soft-ening his persona.

Unfortunately, after his considerable success, he'd decided their small PR firm wasn't big enough and gave his business and incredible chequebook to another company, Madison and Baker, one of their rivals.

Angela remembered how betrayed she'd felt.

"Don't take it so hard," Ronald had told her one night over Chinese takeout. "You know how business is."

"But I helped get him to where he is."

"Only partly. Reemer's the kind of guy who would have succeeded no matter what."

Angela knew her fiancé was right. She knew there was talent behind that smile and a shrewd mind, but she couldn't help feeling hurt. After working closely with Damon for years he hadn't even said 'good job' or 'great working with you'. He just left. But that was how the men in her life seemed to be. She'd helped Ronald get his fledging graphic design firm off the ground and the moment he had no use for her or their child he'd moved to Chicago with his new girlfriend.

Angela felt the tears gather and this time let them fall. It wasn't fair. She stared at Damon's picture with envy. Everything about his life was blessed—from his great looks to his good fortune.

While she was tired and sad. Just like her mother had been.

She covered her face and sobbed.

"No, don't do that," a voice said.

Angela gasped recognizing the low, deep voice. *It couldn't be him.*

"Why are you crying?" he asked, his deep voice echoing his concern.

It was him. She lifted her head, but didn't turn. She couldn't. She didn't want to see him. Not now. Not like this.

What was he doing here? Of all the days why was he here now?

He shifted to look at her face. "Tell me what's wrong."

She took a deep breath then slowly turned and saw the black and white photo behind her come to life.

CHAPTER FOUR

"*A*ngela?" Damon said shocked. "What are you doing here?" Before she could reply, his gaze swept her figure. "Wait, you need to sit down." Again not giving her a chance to say anything he took her elbow and led her to a bench. Angela sat, grateful, because she wasn't sure how much longer she would have remained standing. It had only been two years since she'd last seen him, but the way their relationship had ended made it feel much longer. He hadn't changed much. Not that she'd expected him to. He was still gorgeous, but there was something different.

First his clothes were ordinary, from the light blue jeans he wore to the red and green baseball cap that sat low over his forehead. The Damon she knew from the past always took the time to look ready for the cover of a magazine. And the stubble on his chin was a surprise. He was usually clean shaven, although she had to admit the stubble did nothing to lessen his appeal it only gave him a more rugged, sexier look.

Then there were his eyes—his secret weapon. He could gaze at a woman and make her feel like the most beautiful object in the room. In the past she'd dismissed that ability, but at that moment she found herself falling under his spell as his dark brown eyes reflected a tender concern. Something she hadn't expected from him.

"Are you okay?" he asked again. "Do you need me to get you something?"

"No," Angela said quickly. "I'm all right."

Damon looked at a loss for something else to say which also struck her as odd; he was never at a loss for words. "Congratulations. You and Ronald must be very happy. How is old Ronald? I only met him twice, once at a party at a friend's restaurant, but I remember him clearly. He was a great—"

"He dumped me," Angela cut in before Damon could sing his praises.

"Bastard," Damon finished lamely.

Angela couldn't help a smile, knowing that hadn't been what he'd been prepared to say. "Yes, that's about right."

Damon cleared his throat and briefly glanced away to look around. "So what are you working on? I didn't realize we were doing a campaign for the program, but I haven't been on top of everything lately."

He thought she was working on a campaign. That was perfect. He didn't have to know the truth. She could tell him that was the reason why she was there and then leave and never see him again.

Angela opened her mouth to lie when she heard running footsteps. She glanced up and saw Trish Meadowoods running towards her. Trish was another student in the class. Her long legs ate up the distance and her long brown hair swung wildly in a ponytail behind her.

She halted right in front of them and gasped for breath, her pale face red from exertion. "Oh, good. I'm so glad you haven't left yet." She held out a jacket. "You forgot your coat in the class and it's so cold out I know you need it."

Angela reluctantly took it from her. "Thank you."

"I'm really sorry how that jerk talked to you. Talk about a diva. But we all know he looks down on us. He's a real a—"

"Yes," Angela said sensing Damon's tense energy beside her. "I'm okay now."

"I know you need this program just like the rest of us. There are only a few more weeks left. I'm sure they could think of something else for you to do. They can't just kick you out, it's almost the holidays and I know you want to get out of that basement place you're staying in."

"Yes," Angela agreed, wishing Trish would leave and regretting that she'd shared so much about herself. That was not usually her way.

Trish glanced at Damon then turned back to Angela and nodded. "I'll call you later okay?"

"Okay."

Trish started to turn then paused and stared back at Damon. That's when Angela noticed he'd kept his head lowered the entire time. Trish cocked her head to the side and pointed at him. "Aren't you...?"

He slowly lifted his head. "Yep."

Trish fell onto her knees like a groupie meeting her idol. "Oh my God! This is incredible! I love you!! Could I get an autograph?" She frantically looked around. "Damn, I don't have any paper. Could you—"

"Trish, is that your name?"

"Yes," she said, her eyes full of worship.

"I'll be back and I'll make sure to give you an autograph, but right now I'm busy," he said sending a significant glance at Angela.

She sent Angela a quick look then rushed to her feet. "Yes, of course. Right. Bye."

"Bye," Angela said then watched Trish jog away.

She looked down and realized Damon still held her hand. He absently rubbed his thumb over the back of her palm. It was a tender and natural gesture for him, but affected her more than she wanted it to. It didn't surprise her that he'd be at ease touching a woman. He always knew the right thing to do to make a woman feel comfortable, but she didn't want to be comfortable with him. Unfortunately, she couldn't pull away without drawing attention to herself.

"Why are you in my program?" he asked. He made it sound like a casual question, but she knew it wasn't.

Angela kept her tone light. "Just curious. Well, I'd better get going. I know you came here for a reason and I'd hate to ruin your schedule." She began to stand.

He didn't release her hand forcing her to stay seated. "People don't join out of curiosity. Do I have to repeat my question?"

Angela bit her lip and stared straight ahead.

"Trish mentioned you staying in a basement. Why?"

Angela met his gaze and knew she could no longer lie to him. "Because I live there."

"Why?"

"Why do you think? Because I have nowhere else to go."

"But that doesn't make any sense. What about your job? Have you contacted Ronald? He should be helping you."

"It's a long story. Please, I really have to go."

Damon's tone hardened. "You're not going anywhere until I understand what's going on."

It was too much. First Ricardo showed her how much of a failure she was and now him. A wave of grief, shame and despair threatened to drown her. She lowered her head and burst into tears.

Damon swore then gathered her in his arms. "Shh, I'm sorry. I didn't mean to shout. I just...it doesn't matter," he said sounding helpless.

Angela didn't move, reveling in his strength and comfort. She briefly shut her eyes wanting to melt into his arms. His broad shoulders felt like an anchor against the storm and waves of her life. He smelled good like sweet sugar cane and fresh guava. He smelled like home. For a long moment, Damon didn't say anything then he stood, lifting her up with him. "Come on. Let's go."

She sniffed and wiped her eyes. "Didn't you come here for something?"

"I wanted to speak to Serena but I'll talk to her later."

"Where are we going?"

"Away from here." Damon stepped back and grabbed her coat. "You're going to tell me everything," he said as he helped her put on her coat. He met her gaze, his dark eyes piercing hers. "And you better not lie to me."

CHAPTER FIVE

He couldn't believe it. He was seeing her again. But was it a dream or a nightmare? He wasn't sure which. All he knew was that he never thought he would see her again. Angela Watkins. He remembered the first time he saw her—cool, cultured, beautiful and totally unimpressed by him, but determined to make him a success. At the time he was used to charming every woman in his path and he'd intended to do the same with her.

But one look into her clever brown eyes and he knew he'd met a challenge. For the first time in his life a woman put him off balance. She had skin that reminded him of the desert sands of the Sahara and regal features as though she'd descended from the line of Nefertiti and her dark brown hair was pulled back with a woven silver headband, giving her an air of elegance.

"I'm going to be blunt with you," she said. "My boss doesn't expect much from us. You're attractive, which will make promoting you easy and you have great cooking skills which has made you a minor celebrity. The national market is saturated and more people fizzle than pop so we're going to have to work hard to make you stand out. But I'm going to make you bigger than you could ever imagine."

She was bold and daring and did everything she said she would. Within a couple of years he was known worldwide and he had her to thank for it. But as time passed he grew uneasy with how attached he'd become to her. Her opinions started to mean too much to him, he grew too accustomed to the sound of her voice, eager for her company and he'd even been a little jealous when she'd become engaged to Ronald, but he'd quickly cured himself of that disease by dating a striking Ghanaian doctor named Naki.

But in spite of his effort to distance himself, he knew he was getting too attached and Damon Reemer didn't attach himself to anyone, not even in business. Unfortunately, at the time, he'd allowed others to stroke his ego and convince him that he didn't need her services anymore. He'd mentioned this to his brother just before he attended a conference in England only to return and discover his brother had taken his empty boast seriously.

Leo had cancelled the contract with Angela's company and signed with their rival Madison and Baker. Unfortunately, Damon had forgotten that he had given him the authority to do so. But he hadn't meant what he'd said and after a bitter fight with his brother, he had tried to contact Angela and explain. She refused to deal with him. He sent flowers that were returned wilted and gifts unopened. After weeks of trying, he gave up, moved on and convinced himself that everything was for the best. He reclaimed his freedom, which was everything to him.

At times he wished he'd been more clever at handling the situation, but later told himself it was just business. He'd imagined that she went on to conquer the world, started her own business or became a celebrity consultant. But never this.

He stole a glance at her as she sat in his BMW, still unable to believe what he was seeing. She was still beautiful and elegant. Damon couldn't believe she was in his Apprentice Program. But what stunned him most was how happy he was to see her. To be sitting beside her. He remembered holding her and inhaling her sweet scent and her soft form.

He silently swore, feeling foolish. He wouldn't make too much out of it. He was just relieved that he'd gotten away from him mother and brother—that was all.

Damon drove Angela to a small cozy restaurant he liked to frequent not far out of town. A place where he could dine incognito and enjoy himself.

"What would you two like to drink?" the waiter, a stocky man with average features, asked once they'd settled into a booth. He smiled at Damon, use to his patronage.

"I'd like lime soda," Angela said.

"And I'd like some black coffee," Damon said.

The waiter nodded pleased then hesitated.

Damon noticed the hesitation. "What is it?"

He frowned then looked at Angela before returning his gaze to him. "Um, Cleveland's here."

Damon didn't need to turn to know the person he was talking about. Cleveland was a regular who spent most of the time in the restaurant to keep warm and be around people. "So, do the usual."

"But he brought a friend this time," the waiter whispered.

"It's all right, just add it to my bill."

The waiter nodded with relief then said, "I'll be back with your orders."

Angela frowned. "What was that about? Who's Cleveland?"

"See the guy in the last booth with the orange, brown and white jacket?"

Angela looked past him then nodded. "Yes."

"That's Cleveland."

"Cleveland? What kind of name is that?"

"That's where he's from. He used to own a bar, but he's fallen on hard times and I cover his meals whenever he comes. The management knows to take care of him even when I'm not around."

She returned her gaze to him and blinked. "Oh."

"You sound surprised."

"I am surprised."

Damon ran a tired hand down his face. "I'm not completely heartless."

Angela's gaze shifted from surprise to concern. "Is there something wrong?"

Everything was wrong but he didn't want to talk about it. "No, besides we're not here to talk about me. Tonight's about you. What happened?"

Angela glanced down at the menu and toyed with the plastic sheet that was peeling off. "It doesn't matter."

"It matters to me."

She lifted her gaze. "That's a surprise. I didn't realize you cared."

"I'm sorry how things ended between us."

The waiter returned with their drinks and quickly left when Damon said they needed more time.

Angela opened her menu and stared at the selection. "It was just business," she said in a flat tone.

"I'm not proud of what happened. I don't blame you for hating me."

"I wanted you to drop dead," she admitted.

Damon pushed his menu aside unable to stop a bitter smile. "Well, just wait a few months and you'll get your wish."

CHAPTER SIX

*A*ngela frowned. "That's not very funny."

"I know."

She looked at him for a moment. "You're serious?"

"About dying?" He nodded. "Yes."

"But...you look great."

The ghost of a grim smile touched his lips. "Thanks. I'm really working on not looking like the walking dead."

Her frown increased. "I didn't mean it like that." She sighed. "I don't know exactly how I meant it."

"You meant to say that I don't look like a man who's at death's door."

"Damon—"

"Whose time is running out."

"Damon."

"Who will soon be face-to-face with the Grim Reaper."

"Will you cut that out?"

He sighed. "Sorry, I was on a role."

Angela hesitated, not sure how to proceed. She'd wished a lot of things when he'd dumped her firm for their competitor's:

A nasty sexually transmitted infection from one of his gorgeous girlfriends, a terrible investment that led to bankruptcy (which later had him crawling back to her, begging her to help him restart his career) even a nasty kitchen fire that destroyed all his lovely tools. But she'd never imagined this. Never wished for him to die. "Are you sure?" she said in a soft voice. "Have you gotten a second opinion?"

"Yes and yes. I have about eighteen months. Isn't that great?" He smiled without humor. "Not quite a full two years but close."

"What did your family say?"

"They don't know."

Her brows shot up. "You haven't told them?"

"No and don't plan to."

"Why not?"

"They make my life hardly bearable when I'm healthy I don't want them to make my last year a burden."

"Who else knows?"

He paused for a moment before he said barely above a whisper, "You're the first person I've told."

"I'd like to say I'm touched, but I'm not. It's terribly sad."

"But what I deserve?"

"I'd never think that." She hesitated. "Why are you telling me?"

He shrugged, briefly lowering his gaze. "I don't know..." He lifted his gaze to hers. "Maybe because we both didn't end up living life as we'd planned."

She sighed. "Right."

"But you have a second chance."

"I just lost that."

Damon leaned forward suddenly eager. "Not if you marry me."

She sat back. "What?"

"Marry me. I could provide for you and your baby and—"

"No."

He blinked, surprised. "That was quick. You haven't heard me out yet."

"My answer won't change. I don't want to marry you."

"Listen, when..." He paused then tried again. "When things get bad, I'll go somewhere else. You won't have to take care of me or anything, if that's what's bothering you. This marriage would only be for appearances and—"

Angela shook her head. "Find someone else."

Damon fell quiet for a moment before he said, "You hate me that much?"

She briefly closed her eyes, pained. "I don't hate you."

"Then why won't you hear me out? I'm offering you money, a place to stay, and—" He stopped when she shook her head. She still had her eyes closed, but her refusal was clear. "Why?"

She opened her eyes and for a moment he wished she hadn't. It would have been easier if she did hate him, but the sadness, pity and regret shining in her soft brown gaze was almost his undoing. "I can't accept. It's..." She leaned forward her voice urgent. "Why would you choose me? Me of all people? The last person you should...it doesn't make sense. Why would you do this to yourself? When you don't have much time you should spend it with people who really care about you, not living a lie to impress them."

He lowered his eyes, his voice grew soft. "It won't make me happy."

"And you think this will?"

He met her gaze. "I know it will."

"I don't believe you." She stood. "I'm sorry."

"At least think it over."

"Take care of yourself."

"Is that supposed to be ironic?"

"No." She rested a hand on his shoulder. "I mean it. Find someone who will truly be there for you."

He felt the weight of her hand leave his shoulder. It felt like a greater loss than even her refusal. He lifted his drink and took a long swallow letting the cool, fizzy liquid cover his tongue. It took him a moment to realize he'd ordered coffee. He'd picked up Angela's soda by accident.

Didn't matter now. He took another long swallow before he set the glass down and sighed.

Find someone who will truly be there for you. "I thought I had," he said in a whisper.

Damon pushed back his baseball cap and rubbed his forehead. He probably shouldn't have sprung the idea on her like that. But it had only just come to him. Angela would have been perfect to foil his mother's plans. But she hadn't given him a chance to explain.

But he was lying. It wasn't just for appearances. He didn't want to die alone. She wasn't a stranger to him. He didn't need her to care, but he knew she wouldn't hover over him either. He also wanted to feel like he could pay her back after he'd hurt her.

A chance at redemption.

A chance she'd refused him.

CHAPTER SEVEN

She'd almost said yes.

For an infinitesimally small moment that could hardly register, she'd briefly, crazily, thought of saying 'yes'. The 'no' that had burst from her lips hadn't been quick or well thought out. It had been in response to her traitorous thoughts. Of course she couldn't marry him.

Of course she couldn't pretend to be his wife. Of course she couldn't let him reenter her life and risk trusting him again.

It was ridiculous.

But what was also ridiculous was racing out of the restaurant when Damon had driven her there. Angela silently swore as she held the collar of her coat tight while a fierce cold wind swept past her. Because she hadn't been thinking clearly, she now had to walk to a bus stop and wait for the bus to take her back to the parking lot where she'd left her car. She didn't have money in her budget to catch a ride. Fortunately the bus stop was only a few blocks away.

She couldn't go back.

Besides, the cold air felt good—invigorating. The restaurant had been too warm and the exercise was good for her. She proudly patted her stomach. For both of them.

Angela lifted her head and steeled her heart. Leaving the DRCA building with him had been a mistake, but he'd caught her at a vulnerable moment. She wouldn't let herself be vulnerable again. Not with him. She couldn't take the risk. She knew how dangerous he could be.

He was still tempting and clever. But he'd betrayed her. Not only had he dropped her as his marketer without warning, not only had he gone to their rival company, he'd ruined her reputation at the firm. After what happened, within the company she'd become branded 'the one that let Damon Reemer get away' so when they decided to restructure and increase profit with layoffs she was let go with little sympathy. Luckily, Ronald had helped her find another marketing job through a contact of his. She'd been so grateful to Ronald for that.

It hurt that all she'd done for Damon had been forgotten by him and the firm. He'd unceremoniously dropped her— ignoring her calls and emails—and then weeks (not days) later tried to explain.

She couldn't forgive him for that. There could have been a better way to tell her that he'd outgrown her, she knew that day would come, but he'd taken the coward's way out.

He'd ruined her life and now he wanted to fix it. She wouldn't give him the pleasure. She would fix her own life. How cunning it had been to almost get her to surrender like this, but he'd find someone else. He was never alone.

Just wait a few months and you'll get your wish.

He was dying. How could the man she wanted to hate

most in the world make her feel so sad? Perhaps it was the expression on his face. The vulnerability in his dark brown eyes. She had rarely seen it. Only twice before. His unspoken plea tugged at her heart, but she couldn't—wouldn't bend. Marrying him was too much of a risk.

She wanted to hate him from a distance. Use him as a motivation to better her life. She wanted to remember him how he used to be. Ambitious, savvy and a little ruthless. There was no victory in using a dying man's last days for her own gain. Marrying a man for money, that was not something she could be proud of. Plus keeping a secret from his family, lying to them every day, would be unbearable.

Did he really think she wanted to benefit from his pain, his desperation?

But for a brief, wicked moment she'd thought of it. It could solve all her problems. She could move out of the basement, she wouldn't have to work, her son would have all that he needed.

Angela sat on the hard bench at the bus stop and sighed.

If she'd gone along with his scheme then she'd have to trust a man she'd promised she'd never trust again. What if he changed his mind? What if he left her out in the cold as he did last time? She couldn't risk it.

But that wasn't her biggest fear.

That fear was much worse.

She was afraid that she would grow to care. That she would worry about him. She couldn't afford to worry about anyone. She would find another job and forget his ridiculous request.

He'd shared enough about his family to know why he didn't want to tell them. She knew his brother, Leo, and

Damon's brief mentions of his mother made Angela's mother sound like Pollyanna. She wouldn't miss entering his world again.

She'd made the right choice, Angela told herself, gripping her hands together as she tasted the salty sting of her tears.

CHAPTER EIGHT

A visit from his mother could be one of two things: as sweet as treacle or as appetizing as cod liver oil. Damon had managed to reschedule his mother's 'surprise' visit for the following afternoon, but he didn't dread it any less.

He loved her, more out of habit than inclination, but when he pressed a kiss on her cheek, he wished he'd been clever enough to come up with a reason to reschedule for another month (or three).

They sat in the living room—heaven forbid they sit in the kitchen. She avoided it like it was her kryptonite. She took no pleasure in food and even less pleasure in anything Damon ever tried to prepare for her. He'd stopped trying to please her at thirteen when she'd taken one bite of his curried rice and thrown the rest away.

Any mention of Popa irritated her and any type of culinary discussions bored her.

Presently she was using a knife and fork to nibble her way through the four organic strawberries she'd allowed him to serve her. He sighed as he watched her take a tiny bite. Just once he wished he'd see her finish a strawberry in two bites instead of ten.

"You look pale," said the reed thin, brown skinned woman sitting in front of him, her bony knees peeking out from her suede skirt. Her dark hair was swept back in a French knot, which only enhanced her striking features.

"I'm fine, Mom." He cleared his throat. "At least let me drizzle some cream on your—"

"Why ruin what's already perfect?" she said taking another little bite, her soft island accent almost making her words sound reasonable.

He rubbed his chin knowing he shouldn't be dreaming of shoving two strawberries in her mouth and forcing her to swallow.

"I'm glad to hear that you're fine because, simply put, I'm not *fine*. Far from it." She stabbed a wafer thin slice and popped it in her mouth.

"I'm sorry to hear that."

She sent him a look. "You don't sound sorry."

He shrugged. "Probably because I have no idea what I've done wrong."

"What do you mean you don't want to meet Vanessa?"

"Exactly what I said."

"But she's perfect for you."

"I seriously doubt that," he mumbled. The women his mother chose for him tended to be completely imperfect matches. They were either beautiful and boring. Cute and impractical or women who could not form opinions unless he gave it to them. Naturally those were the type of women his mother preferred since she didn't like anyone who contradicted her. Some men wanted to grow up and marry a woman just like their mother. He was not one of those men.

She set her fork down with a click. "What did you say?"

"Nothing."

She shot him a look. "That's what I thought." She cleared her throat. "At least give Vanessa a try. She's different than the others."

"How different?"

His mother pulled out her cell phone and showed him an image on her screen.

For a moment he blinked. He saw a picture of a mousy looking black woman, with her shag of unstyled hair hanging around her face dressed in a shabby brown sweater-set that had probably never been in fashion. Definitely not his type. Certainly not his mother's type either.

He started to laugh. He would enjoy this little game.

His mother frowned.

"Okay, this is it," he said with delight. "This is her. You finally understand me."

"Damon."

"I'll go out with her."

She stared at him. "You're not serious."

"Aren't you?" he said in challenge. If she thought he'd back down from this she was wrong. After being turned down by Angela he was game for anything.

His mother looked at the picture again before she faced him. She took a moment to recover herself, but Jeannie Branson always recovered. "She's highly accomplished—"

He rested his chin in his hands. "Of course she is."

"You can't stand her up. Or cancel at the last minute."

He grinned. "I wouldn't dream of it."

CHAPTER NINE

But he briefly thought about it when the day arrived. He'd made a reckless choice, but he'd been making a bunch of them lately including the disastrous proposal to Angela a week ago. However, when you didn't have much time left you didn't tend to ruminate over things too much.

One blind date would be a good diversion and get his mother off his case at least for a little while.

He arrived early at the cozy yet playfully styled restaurant that served American food with a Mediterranean accent to a client base used to spending lots of money. There were enough CEOs and politicians and their families that no one paid him any notice. He'd also chosen the place because while he could take a bad date, he could not take a bad *dinner* date. Food mattered too much to him. He was very particular where he ate—the atmosphere was welcoming, the waitstaff expertly trained—and was known for their garden fresh vegetables and seasonal dishes. He already knew he'd order crisp calamari as a starter and would recommend the housemade ravioli stuffed with wild mushrooms if Vanessa was so inclined.

He was considering the wine to order when something brown and trembling caught his eye. He looked up and saw Vanessa the moment she walked through the restaurant's glass doors. She looked as scared as a mouse in a room full of cats and as sexy as a piece of cardboard. She wore a shapeless black coat over a long brown skirt that reached past her ankles and a brown sweater, which looked like they might have swallowed her breasts because he couldn't see them.

He waved. She hurried over to him and sat down before he could ask if he could take her coat.

She mumbled something.

He leaned forward. "I'm sorry?"

She tucked a strand of black hair behind her ear and mumbled again.

He leaned forward a little more. "I didn't get that either. You're going to have to speak up."

"I didn't mean to keep you waiting," she said.

"No, problem, I was early." He gestured to the food on the table. "I already ordered appetizers. They just arrived."

She mumbled something, he imagined she said 'good' or 'thank you' he didn't really care which.

The conversation went downhill from there. He'd ask questions then she'd mumble a reply.

Fortunately, the food was delicious; the chardonnay cream sauce on his ravioli was divine.

Vanessa ordered lamb shank and ate it with all the pleasure of a woman forced to eat a leather sole. He inwardly sighed. If she'd at least pretended to enjoy the food the game would have been a lot more fun, but it had become tedious. When she ate her banana bread pudding with vanilla ice cream (or rather took three bites of it before letting the ice cream melt into the pudding) he finally gave up. "You can stop the act."

She looked at him startled. "Act?"

The startled expression pleased him—not as much as the Sicilian almond cake he'd just finished—but few things could compete with a decadent dessert that included toasted almonds, a hint of grated lemon rind enhancing, rather than overpowering, the sugar and flour in a cake baked to perfection. "Yes, the costume," he motioned to her clothes, "and the voice. Relax, you win. I'm not interested. Now you can be yourself."

She narrowed her eyes.

His eyes met hers with mischief. "You think I don't know what you're up to? You're a beautiful woman. The mousy hairstyle and dumpy clothes can't hide that, although that enormous sweater does a pretty good job and that voice is beyond ridiculous. You'd sound louder if you mimed everything. We both don't want to be here, so let's just enjoy ourselves."

She stared at him for a long moment then straightened her stooped shoulders and sighed. "So I didn't fool you at all, huh?"

"Your disguise was very clever. But I know how to look at raw ingredients and see beauty."

Vanessa sighed again. "It's nothing against you."

Damon gasped as if wounded. "And here I thought I was special."

She studied him for a moment. "Why did you decide to go out with me?"

"I was curious."

"You could really tell it was a joke by my photograph?"

He shook his head. "No, I knew from before."

"Before?"

"I saw you at a club several nights ago."

"You noticed me?"

"I always notice beautiful women."

"And remember them?"

"I remember them when they are dancing with electric hips."

She took a sip of her drink. "I see."

"With another gorgeous woman."

She paused with the glass to her lips. "I'm not— I mean, I was just curious and—"

"You don't need to explain, although it looked pretty serious."

"But I'm not—"

Damon held up his hand. "I don't care."

She sighed. "My mother does."

He nodded. "I know the feeling."

She smiled and for a moment she looked as beautiful as he knew her to be in spite of the disguise. "Thanks for that."

"What?"

"You didn't say, 'Don't worry, she loves you. It will all work out.'"

"I don't like lying to my dates."

"That's good to know. So tell me why you're still single. You know my secret, what's yours?"

"Who says I have one? I'm single because I want to be. It's as simple as that."

"Then how come I get the feeling that you're hiding something from me?"

"Because I hide a lot of things."

Vanessa rested her chin in her hands. "You seem like an okay guy. I have a friend—"

"For a threesome?"

"Not on your life."

He made his lower lip tremble and blinked his eyes as if he was about to cry. "You shouldn't get a man's hopes up like that."

She laughed. "The man's got humor."

"I've got a lot of things that might impress you. Or maybe not. However, a number of women have been impressed by the size of my—"

"I'm not interested."

"—spice collection."

She laughed. "You are a bad boy."

He feigned innocence. "I don't know what you're talking about."

She took a bite of his cake. "Hmm. This is delicious."

"I'm glad you think so since you've wasted your banana pudding."

She looked down at her plate. "I'm sure it's still fine."

"Fine as anything can be after sitting under a faint restaurant light at room temperature mixing with melted ice cream."

"You make it sound like a tragedy."

"Because it is."

Vanessa shook her head amused. "I know you're a chef, but I thought it was just a job, not an obsession. I didn't realize food meant this much to you."

Damon placed a hand on his chest. "Food is my life." He stopped her from taking another bite of his cake. "Which is why I'm going to order you your own dessert."

She pointed at his cake. "You don't like to share your life?"

"No."

"You're going to have to one day."

"Perhaps, but not today."

She set her fork down. "Fair enough." She picked up a

spoon and scooped up the pudding and ice cream. "It's not half bad." When he made a face she scooped up more. "Here, try some."

He shivered. "The delight is all yours."

"Your loss." She took another bite. "I really dreaded this date. I'm glad I got to meet you."

"Same."

She took a deep breath. "What are you going to tell your mother?"

"That we had a fabulous time and I want to see you again."

Her face fell.

"But you turned me down."

Her face lit up. "You'd do that for me?"

"Of course." He chewed his lip. "But it won't solve anything. If your mother is anything like mine, she won't stop."

"I know. But right now this is working."

"Until it doesn't," he said in a grim tone.

"Right." She took out her business card. "But I won't worry about that right now."

He took the card and read: Dr. Vanessa Brand, internist. "Why so formal?"

"It just feels right."

"You need new patients?"

"No, the truth is I would like to see you again. As friends."

"You know how to reach me. But you might regret it."

"Why?"

"I like to show off my enormous—"

"Spice collection?"

He playfully wiggled his eyebrows, glad she'd caught on to his teasing. "—to all my friends."

"All of them? Not just the special ones?"

He winked. "The special ones get samples."

"Then I hope to become a dear friend."

"I don't imagine that will be hard."

She smiled then it slowly faded. "You're not at all what I'd imagined you to be. You're so easy to be with and talk to there has to be someone—"

"I told you. Food is my life. My mother hasn't learned that yet."

"I understand." She paused. "You won't ever let slide that I was with—"

"None of my business."

"Even as a friend?"

"Especially as a friend. Your life is yours and my life is mine."

She released a sigh of relief. "If there's ever a favor you need, let me know."

For a moment he thought of asking her the same question he'd asked Angela, but the words got caught in his throat. Vanessa would be suitable. A comfortable pretend wife. They would both help each other out. But something stopped him. Somehow he didn't want to tell her that he was dying. That he was afraid of being alone, it felt too personal somehow.

Telling Angela had felt more natural. He couldn't explain why. Maybe he was overthinking it. Maybe it was his guilt talking. He needed to forget about her. Vanessa would be perfect. A beautiful doctor. The plan was foolproof.

He chewed his lip. "Actually, there is something you could do for me."

"What?"

He swallowed. "My family doesn't know this but—"

"Somebody help!" a woman cried.

They turned and saw a frantic mother shaking her lifeless toddler.

anessa rushed over. "What happened?"

"I think he's choking," the mother said. "I don't know what to do."

The baby's face was already turning blue.

The father panicked, the mother cried.

Vanessa deftly took over.

The restaurant at once noisy became as silent as a cemetery.

Damon feared the baby was dead. Too much time had passed, but Vanessa kept working and finally a large piece of meat popped out and landed on the floor.

The crowd cheered. The parents thanked her.

Damon and Vanessa returned to their seats.

"The meal is on the house," the waiter said.

"No, please," Vanessa said embarrassed. "It's my job."

But the waiter wouldn't hear of it and left the table taking the bill.

"You're a hero," Damon said with pride.

She looked suddenly shy. "It was training coming in. But

before that what were you going to tell me?"

He could be reckless, but something stopped him. Why did he briefly wish Angela was sitting there? Why did he feel like calling her and telling her what he'd just seen?

He glanced down at his plate; he'd have no trouble sharing dessert with her, he'd done it before. Angela's idea not his. They'd gone to a new restaurant for a business meeting and when he'd bitten into the vanilla cake he'd ordered for dessert and it tasted crispy, he was infuriated.

He held up his hand. "Waiter?"

Angela looked at him alarmed. "What's the matter?"

"This cake is disgusting."

"Put your hand down."

"No. They need to know about this." He snapped his fingers. "Waiter."

She took a bite of the cake. "The bottom's a little burnt, but it's hardly disgusting."

"Did you just hear yourself? The bottom is black. Where is that waiter?"

She lifted the corner of the cake to see the bottom. "It's a little brown, but hardly black. Stop exaggerating."

"This is unacceptable. Waiter!"

Their server hustled over to them. "I'm sorry. Is there a problem?"

"Yes," Damon said.

"No," Angela countered.

The waiter looked at them confused, a slow wave of red rising up his skinny neck.

"We're sorry to bother you," she said.

"I'm not—" Damon stopped and winced when she kicked him.

"It's okay."

The waiter nodded and left the table.

Before Damon could speak, Angela pinned him with a stare and said in a low voice, "This is a new restaurant and you will not destroy them."

His brows shot up. "Who's exaggerating now?"

"Have you forgotten who you are? Just imagine if you call the chef and loudly proclaim your dissatisfaction for others to hear. You're not an every day, ordinary patron. Or even your father's son. You're Damon Reemer. You have power. I should know. I've helped you build it. I want you to be a little more careful next time. You will not complain, you will keep your opinion to yourself. Understood?"

His jaw twitched. "But—"

She narrowed her eyes. "Understood?"

He folded his arms and nodded.

She pushed her plate towards him. "This isn't bad."

He made a face. "That isn't exactly high praise. The bottom of this cake could be used as surface cleaner."

She kicked him.

He glared at her and rubbed his shin. "Stop that."

"Do you know how to keep your thoughts to yourself?"

"Yes," he said in a dark voice. "Very well. Right now you have no idea what I think of you."

Angela laughed. "I have a pretty good idea." She took his cake and pointed to the fudge she'd given him. "Try it."

He sighed before he did so. To his annoyance it was good. He watched her take another bite of the cake.

"How can you continue to eat that?"

"It can grow on you. The smoky aftertaste is unique. Add a little rum and it might work."

"Stop eating it."

"No. It's edible."

Damon smashed it with the palm of his hand. "Now it's not."

Angela stared at him. "What was that for?"

"Watching you endure that was getting on my nerves," he said, calmly wiping his hand with a cloth napkin. "You can share my dessert."

She grinned amused. "It really bothered you that much?"

"More than you know." He cut the fudge in half. "Go on."

She took a bite. "It really wasn't that—"

"Don't say it."

"But it's the truth. When I was growing up we had this old finicky toaster that if you didn't force it to pop at the right moment it would burn the toast. Once I forgot and it basically turned the bread to charcoal, but there was no bread left and I was hungry and I learned that enough butter and jam could solve a crisis."

He blinked. "That's one of the saddest stories I've ever heard."

She laughed at his expression. "It's not tragic."

He shook his head. "Tell me another story like that and I could burst into tears."

"Come on. You've never had to eat anything burnt?"

"Not willing, no."

"A friend or girlfriend has never—"

"No. And if they had I wouldn't eat it. Food is too important to me."

She'd laughed again and he remembered the buoyant sound even now. It always lifted his mood no matter how low he felt.

But she wasn't there. And he knew his final days would be more of this. Hiding the truth. But his life had already been like this. It had been filled with relationships that didn't really matter, lots of travel and a crammed schedule that didn't allow him to be alone with his thoughts. He didn't like being alone. It was one of the reasons he'd agreed to the blind date. Otherwise he'd be at home with the loop of 'she'd said no' 'she'd said no' repeating in his mind.

He took a deep breath. While he wasn't used to losing, rejection was something he'd experienced more than he'd care to admit. Usually from those he cared about most. He'd had a childhood of hurtful words to remind him.

But he'd never forgive himself for not chasing after Angela, when he'd realized (too late) that he'd driven her to the restaurant. But by the time he'd figured it out and raced to the nearest bus stop, running so hard and fast he feared his lungs would burst, the bus was pulling away from the curb and merged into traffic while a large truck barreling past, belched fumes in his face.

Damon bent forward, resting his hands on his knees, his heart pounding so fast it hurt. The breathlessness and pain reminded him he wasn't the healthy man he used to be.

He slowly straightened and gazed at the bus as it grew smaller in the distance.

Too late. He'd been too late. Just like in the past when he'd tried to explain what had happened, he'd been too late then too.

But he'd get past this. He didn't have time for regrets. He didn't have much time at all. All that mattered was now. But Vanessa wasn't the answer to his pain.

"It's nothing," he said to Vanessa, embarrassed by his brief lapse in judgment. There was nothing he could freely share with her. "Just that you should tell your mother she has a daughter worth being proud of."

Vanessa was an amazing woman, Damon thought as he

drove home under an ink black night sky. She was perfect for his crazy plan. She wasn't interested in him and he wasn't interested in her. She was a medical professional so she wouldn't be shaken with what he had to deal with. He liked her, they got on well.

But that night he dreamt about someone else—a beautiful woman with a bright laugh and teasing eyes—and wished he'd been able to convince her to stay with him in more ways than one.

CHAPTER ELEVEN

ngela was actually thinking about Damon the night she went into labor.

It had been a week since she'd last seen him. A week since he'd held her in his arms. He'd hugged her before years ago, but those hugs were always quick and friendly. They hadn't been like the day he'd held her close to his body and almost convinced her that he would protect her with his life.

But she angrily pushed the thought from her mind as she tidied up her place. Damon was the last person she had the luxury to think about. It was November and she'd have to come up with a good reason not to celebrate Thanksgiving with Megan and her mother this year. Most years they celebrated at Angela's place (although she didn't cook, Megan and her mother came loaded with delicious food) with Ronald in attendance. She wasn't ready to explain his absence to her mother yet.

Damon had to stay out of her mind. She had too much to do and she didn't feel well.

Her back had been bothering her most of the day as she tried to figure out what her next step should be.

She tried not to think about his soothing hand on hers, his warm brown eyes. She needed a job. Not a man. Certainly not a man like him. She went to bed that night in a foul mood and woke up thinking she'd eaten something bad. She had the worse stomachache ever.

She went to the toilet wondering how baked plantain and red beans and rice could upset her so much. She hadn't eaten that much. She sat on the toilet. And groaned. This was like no stomachache she'd ever had before. She rubbed the side of her stomach and swore when it tightened.

It contracted in a way she'd never felt before.

Wait...contracted?

It was a contraction?

She jumped up from the seat, panic gripping her as tightly as the contraction had.

No. No. No. This couldn't be happening. She wasn't ready yet. She thought about the calendar carefully arranged on her fridge. She had two weeks to go. Two weeks to get ready. Two weeks to be prepared. Two more precious weeks to...

She gripped the side of the sink when another contraction seized her. She took a deep breath. She wouldn't panic. Panic would make it worse. Perhaps it was a false alarm. It had to be. She couldn't go into labor.

She took two more deep breaths then stared at the frightened face in the mirror. She could handle this. Mind over matter. She would be okay.

She took another deep, steadying breath feeling the scared tension leave her body. Her mind would get her through this.

She walked to the living room and gently sat down on the couch.

Calm and controlled.

That's what she was known for. That was who she needed to be. She closed her eyes.

That calm collected woman had a job tomorrow. A job she needed. A job she couldn't lose. She'd convinced a friend of Serena to let her design her website and she already had a bunch of ideas. That job could lead to others. She needed time.

She needed two more weeks.

And with that thought the pain seemed to fade into the past. She was safe. She smiled, resting a hand on her stomach. "Thank you little one for giving me a little more time," she whispered. "When you come I'll do everything I can for you."

With renewed hope she stood and walked to her bedroom and she almost made it before another contraction nearly brought her to her knees.

Fear replaced panic.

Despair replaced hope.

Tears fell.

She wasn't going to make it.

She wasn't going to get her two weeks. Serena's friend would find someone else. She wouldn't get the job or the money. Her fledging career had died before it had even begun.

It wasn't supposed to happen this way. She wasn't supposed to go into labor in this shabby basement apartment with no job. She wasn't supposed to be alone like this. Her life continued to go in directions she didn't plan.

Angela crawled to her bed and grabbed her cell phone and dialed Serena's number.

"I'm sorry to bother you," she said in a choked voice, "but... I need your help."

CHAPTER TWELVE

"I thought he would be bigger," Megan said looking at her new nephew asleep in his crib. His soft breathing as soothing as the pastel colors in the cozy room at the birthing center. It was just the respite Angela needed after ten hours of labor. She thought the pain would swallow the rage she felt at the unfairness that she'd had to give birth alone. That Ronald hadn't been with her.

That no one else had.

Serena was too skittish to stay there with her.

And Angela would have rather ingested a porcupine than have had her sister as her labor coach and she'd never considered her mother who was both too far away without reliable transportation and worrisome (she'd wonder where Ronald was) to think about.

However, the soothing and experienced voice of the midwife helped guide her through the thrilling, scary, exciting trek from mother-to-be to new mom.

Soon pain turned to joy when the high pitched wail of her son sweetened the sweat soaked air. Feeling the soft curls on his head and his tiny wrinkly body, pressed against hers made the journey worthwhile. He was what she'd fought for and who she would continue to fight for. He made living worthwhile.

Where her sister saw flaws, Angela only saw beauty. "He's big enough."

"But you were huge." Megan held her hand out from her own flat stomach to mime the extent Angela's belly had been. "I was at least expecting eight pounds or something. He's positively scrawny."

Angela sent her sister a look. "You don't have to be here you know."

"Of course I do," Megan said, ignoring her sister's sharp tone. "I had to meet my nephew. Don't worry, we'll work on putting weight on him."

Before Angela could tell her sister that she thought her baby was perfect, an older ginger skinned woman with dark brown eyes and a round face, wearing a crooked shoulder length wig entered the room and rushed over to her. "Oh my dear. I'm sorry I'm late."

"You're not late," Angela said as her mother placed a light kiss on her cheek. "I'm glad you're here."

Megan sighed. "And your wig is crooked."

"It is?" Her mother reached up and tried to straighten the wig making it more askew. "I was in such a hurry."

Megan adjusted the wig, an event she and Angela had both grown used to. Since their teens, their mother had hid her hair under wigs, telling them that they saved her time. They knew it was her one luxury, once having a selection of ten. But in her latter years she'd reduced her collection to three—one close cropped grey, another a chin length black one with curls and the final one a sleek medium brown wig with red highlights.

"I don't know why you chose a birthing center instead of a hospital," her mother said, her light island lilt making her words sound more of a criticism than she meant them to be.

Megan stepped back to check how the wig fit then nodded pleased. "Much better."

Her mother absently touched her wig, her brows furrowed in worry. "What if there had been complications?"

Angela forced a smile. She was tired but didn't regret her choice. "I was low risk and everything worked out."

Megan folded her arms. "Personally, if I ever have a baby, I want to be in a hospital, with my lower half as numb as a tree trunk."

Her mother frowned. "Can trunks be numb? I didn't know they could feel."

"It's just a turn of phrase, Mum."

"But I've never heard it before."

"Because I made it up."

"You made it up? Why would you make up something that doesn't make any sense? How can a woman be as numb as a tree trunk?"

Megan rolled her eyes. "I'm just—"

"Positively daft."

Megan rested a hand on her hip. "Now wait—"

"Mum," Angela cut in before the argument could escalate. "Would you like to see him?"

Her mother blinked then her face brightened. "Oh of course. Your sister's foolishness distracted me."

Megan tapped her chest. "My foolishness? You were the one with the crooked wig. This is the thanks I get?"

Her mother ignored her and hurried over to the crib. She gasped with delight at the sight she saw. "He's beautiful."

Megan folded her arms again and sent her sister a look. "He doesn't look anything like you."

Angela sent her sister a glare. "Let me repeat myself. You really don't have to be here."

"Of course he doesn't look like Angela," their mother said. "He looks like Ronald." She suddenly looked around the room as a thought struck her. "Where is he?"

Megan stared at her mother surprised. "You mean you don't know about them?"

Her mother frowned confused. "Know what?"

"That Ronald missed everything because he's traveling," Angela said before her sister could say anything. "He's sorry he couldn't be here."

"Or even have flowers delivered," Megan added, taking note of the room, bare of any gifts.

Angela sent her a foul gesture. Megan grinned.

"Oh, that's a shame," their mother said. "Call him."

Angela's voice broke. "Call him?"

"Yes, so that I can congratulate him."

"It's nighttime there."

"He'll wake up for this."

"I already told him and he's gone back to sleep, I'd hate to bother him again."

"But—"

"Why congratulate him? He hasn't done anything."

"He gave you a son. Besides, it'd be nice to hear his voice." She waved a dismissive hand. "Never mind. I'll speak to him later."

"Right."

"I need to get something to drink." She bustled out of the room.

Megan turned to Angela, her gaze sharp and judgmental. "She doesn't know?"

"She doesn't need to know. At least not yet."

"Then when? He's been out of your life for months now."

"When things are better I'll tell her. She's sick enough."

"She's not *that* sick. Do you see how quickly she moves?"

"I don't want her to worry about me."

Megan rested her hands on her hips. "You want me to do that instead?"

"No," Angela said suddenly feeling very tired. She couldn't fight her sister and didn't want to try. "I'm okay."

"You're afraid she'll be ashamed of you."

Yes, but Angela didn't want to admit it. "I said I'm okay."

Megan nodded, doubtful. "What are you going to do?"

"I've got plans."

She folded her arms. "Tell me."

"I'm tired. I just squeezed out an object the size of a watermelon through a hole the size of a lemon."

Megan shook her head. "Don't exaggerate." She gestured to her nephew. "I've seen papayas bigger than him."

"Go away."

"He's about the size of a tiny pineapple."

"Now."

Megan chuckled to herself before she placed a light kiss her on her sister's cheek. "Congrats, Sis. You'll be a great mom."

Angela inwardly groaned, feeling her heart softening. Just when her sister got on her nerves the most she could be sweet.

Unfortunately, she didn't have long to think about that before her mother returned to the room.

"It's such a shame Ronald couldn't be here. But I am here now and can help you for the next few days. I can stay at your place—"

"No," Angela said with more force than she meant to. But the last thing she wanted was for her mother to see where she lived. "I mean that's not necessary, I already have a friend staying with me who offered to help."

Her mother hesitated. "Are you sure?"

"Positive."

They chatted a little more (very little since Angela and her mother rarely had a lot to say to each other) before her mother left.

With one potential disaster avoided, Angela slept.

WHICH WAS THE MOST SHE'D GET OVER THE NEXT SEVERAL months. If she'd known she would hardly get a straight eight hours of sleep she would have slept longer. She barely remembered the next three months. She noticed neither the change in the months nor the change in the season or the holiday seasonal work at a shipping center, she'd managed to get.

However, she hazily remembered a rather awkward Thanksgiving dinner hosted at Megan's house where Angela created more elaborate reasons to answer her mother's questions as to why they weren't at Angela's house and why Ronald wasn't there.

Weeks flew past her in the haze of surviving life with a newborn, she felt like a zombie. Between sleep deprived headaches, sore nipples and two cancelled prospective website projects, she wasn't sure she'd survive. She loved her little boy to bits but feared he'd be the death of her.

In March, she managed to get a part-time job as a cashier at a dollar store and another part-time job at a convenience store. And they would have been fine if the manager at the dollar store hadn't kept brushing his erection up against her.

It hadn't started out that way—at least not the first week. But by the end of the first month she'd had to grit her teeth and endure his hand grazing her behind on a number of occasions. The second month working there she'd held her tongue when his hand accidentally brushed against her breast—more than once.

But the day when she was at the register and he stopped behind her and reached for something over her shoulder so that she could feel the full force of his erection she knew her days were numbered. It wasn't something she could brush aside and ignore. Her entire body rebelled at the insult in a way that, for a moment, she thought she'd be sick (preferably all over his crisp khaki pants and white shirt).

But she still said nothing. She thought of the woman she paid to look after Jadin. She thought of the money she wanted to save so that she could get out of the basement apartment. It had been a soggy April and rainy May, forcing her and Jadin to try to fall asleep to the mechanical sound of Serena's old sump pump to keep the basement from flooding.

She knew this job was a necessary stepping stone to a better life. She was lucky to have one when so many were still out of work and business was brisk there. It was a job that could last.

She told herself all this as she showered that night and planned ways to avoid him. Ways she could bare it just a little while longer.

The third month, however, was different.

It wasn't just the feel of his erection against her; it was his hot breath on her neck.

She lost her temper and all rational thought fled.

It was the fact that he leaned in so close that she could smell his aftershave. This time her body didn't feel repelled it felt enraged.

She was briefly surprised by the expensive scent. Ronald used the same brand. Maybe if he hadn't reminded her of Ronald she wouldn't have spun around and grabbed his crotch. She wouldn't have glared at his startled wide eyes and tightened her hold.

She wouldn't have said, "What should I spare? Your balls or your dick?" before a customer entered the store and asked for assistance.

She let him go—leaving him bent over in pain, swearing and moaning—and smiled at the customer who cast a nervous look at the man before she stated her question.

She lost her job.

That hadn't surprised her. The reason he'd given was laughable "not a team player" but she knew he didn't really need to give a reason at all.

She thought of charging him with sexual harassment, but didn't have the energy. Besides, she still had a part time job at the convenience store.

Until the convenience store owner decided to hire a family member who was allergic to work. Any job he was given he found a way not to do it. When Angela complained she was fired from that job as well.

But she still had hope that she could do something online. She wanted to use her skills. She wasn't meant to stay as a clerk in a store; she'd gotten a degree so that she could help people with her skills. After a few harrowing weeks working for a staffing company that couldn't give her enough assignments to cover all her expenses she was able to get another website design job for a new start up.

The money wasn't bad either. Nothing like what she use to get but it would cover her for at least two weeks. She'd learned to live day by day, so having a week, let alone two, in which not to worry about money was a welcome change.

The day she finished the project and the money hit her banking account she felt optimistic. She had managed to get herself back. She didn't need anyone's help.

Angela closed her laptop with a satisfied smile and thought about what she'd prepare for dinner as she walked over to Jadin's crib vaguely surprised by how quiet he'd been. It had been a welcome relief but something about his stillness worried her.

She looked down at him and a sliver of ice pierced her heart as she realized he'd stopped breathing.

CHAPTER THIRTEEN

The wail of the ambulance sirens made her panic and grief nearly unbearable.

Only moments ago, with the operator's help over the phone, Angela had followed her instructions and managed to get Jadin gasping, which meant he was still alive, thank goodness, but his breathing was still far from normal, before the medics had finally arrived in what had seemed like hours but likely had only been minutes.

In the ambulance, Angela could barely see all they were doing to him through her sea of tears. How could this be happening? How could his life be over when it had only just begun? Things were finally looking up for them. None of this made sense. He was healthy yesterday. Wasn't he?

And now she was going to a hospital. The last place she wanted to be without insurance. Even before Jadin had been born she'd researched her options: Seeking a hospital that would offer a patient discount if she paid in cash and allowing her to make payments on the cost of her delivery ahead of her due date. She'd also found a doctor who would accept the same. But both would have put her meager savings in the red so she'd chosen the cheaper option of a birthing center and midwife instead.

But all the careful planning, the dedication to Jadin's well-being by providing food and shelter hadn't been enough.

At the hospital Angela tried to answer the doctor's questions as best she could although everything felt jumbled in her mind. Had she missed signs? Had he been sick and she hadn't noticed? The doctor told her something she didn't hear, a nurse touched her arm and said something she couldn't understand. She felt like she was underwater and everything around her was garbled.

There were tests. More questions. Some more tests and then after hours of waiting a diagnosis: Her son had a respiratory infection. Likely caused from the dampness in the apartment and the rainy spring weather.

Guilt nearly choked her. Her pride had put her son's life in jeopardy. But before she could process that thought, they told her he also had a slight tear in his lung that needed to be repaired. The respiratory infection could be dealt with antibiotics but the lungs needed surgery.

The medical bills from the tests and hospital stay alone would sink her, how could she afford surgery on top of that? But he needed treatment. The best. And she'd make sure he got it. She'd find a way.

She pulled out her cell phone and thought of calling her sister then quickly dismissed the idea. She didn't want to be in debt to her.

Angela sighed, feeling the keen weight of her inevitable defeat. She knew of only one person who could help her. It would mean swallowing her pride. She only hoped it wasn't too late for both of them.

CHAPTER FOURTEEN

Damon stood paralyzed at his front door remembering his first wet dream. A beautiful woman had arrived on his doorstep and said, "I'll do anything you ask me to. Just tell me what you want."

Little could he ever have imagined that dream coming true. That one hot spring day Angela Watkins would show up on his doorstep and say those tantalizing words. And not just say them, but mean them. Damon rubbed his thumb against his forefinger until he felt like his skin would catch fire, not quite trusting his hearing.

He hadn't seen her in...what? How long had it been? It had been cold, right? Yes. And she'd been pregnant. He remembered that much even though his mind felt fuzzy. The weather wasn't cold and she definitely wasn't pregnant now. So that made the last time he'd seen her maybe four? Six-seven months ago?

And yet she was here? At his house? Looking at him as if she were willing to get on her knees?

So far, over the last several months, he hadn't experienced

any of the side effects of the new medications he was taking. No headaches, dry mouth, nausea, or depressive thoughts. But perhaps audio hallucinations had been a tiny possible side effect he'd overlooked. He couldn't trust himself.

It was the look of desperation on Angela's face—something not clearly seen by anyone who didn't know her well—that alarmed him. She expertly hid it by the set of her jaw and the steely gaze, but he knew her too well to know that she hadn't shown up at his door unexpected ready to walk away without getting what she'd come for.

That look told him this moment was real.

And very wrong.

"Come inside," he said.

She hesitated then looked at something behind him. "You have company."

He turned to see Vanessa standing in the hallway, unsure. He gave her a nod that he was okay so she returned his nod before she disappeared into another room. She'd come over to share a pizza and watch a goofy movie they'd both been curious about. They were only friends but over the past several month hadn't dissuaded their parents that they weren't something more.

Damon turned back to Angela, resisting the urge to grab the front of his shirt. His heart was racing (another possible side effect he'd never experienced before but she always had that effect on him). "No, she's family."

Her eyes widened. "Of course. So you finally...found someone who... S-s-she's beautiful."

At first he didn't know what she was talking about then realized she probably thought he'd asked Vanessa to marry him, as he had her. He shook his head. "Angela, I'm not—"

"And I didn't even ask how you're doing."

"I'm fine." He motioned her forward. He needed to sit down. He wasn't sure how much longer he could remain standing. "Come in."

"I shouldn't have come. But I'll do anything. I'll clean if you need me to."

Vanessa came up to them. "Is something wrong?"

"No," Angela said. "I was just telling your husband—"

She jerked her head back. "Husband?"

"—that I need some work."

Damon gripped the door handle and said, "And I've been trying to convince her to come inside."

He didn't know whether it was his tone or look, but Vanessa took over. She'd become someone he could depend on. She pulled Angela inside and said, "First we're not married and second you look like you need to sit down. Come with me."

She hustled her down the hall.

Damon closed the door and rested his forehead against it. He took deep, steadying breaths. One...two...three...

He heard Vanessa's cautious footsteps before he felt her light grasp on his arm. "Are you okay?"

He managed a nod.

"You look terrible," Vanessa said. "Who is she?"

"I never thought I'd see her again."

"Do you need me to get rid of her?"

He shook his head.

"But she hurt you, right? I can sense it."

He shook his head again before he turned to her. "No, she didn't. I-I'm just." He forced a smile. "I'll be okay. Has she said anything to you?"

"She just keeps apologizing and telling me that it won't take long."

"What won't take long?"

"You have to find out for yourself. She seems determined to only speak to you, but if you can't handle it—"

"I can handle it. She just surprised me, that's all. Let me talk to her alone." He walked into the formal living room where he found Angela staring at the painting of Popa she'd given him after Popa had died. She'd stopped by his house, since he'd refused to see or speak to her for days. At the time he'd questioned whether he'd wanted to go with the path she'd set for him. He considered stopping everything and just focusing on being a chef in a kitchen again.

He'd expected her to try to convince him to return to work, but she hadn't. She didn't ask to come in and he hadn't offered. Instead she handed him a poster size object wrapped in brown paper before she said, "I'm sorry for your loss," and left.

Damon waited until the next morning before he finally ripped open the brown covering and a burst of orange caught his eye. He quickly removed the rest of the wrapping and found a portrait of Popa standing in front of the exaggerated heat (shown by red and orange flames soaring upward from a stove) of a kitchen, holding a knife like a samurai, wearing a crisp white chef's jacket that complemented the rich brown of his smooth, clean shaven face and he wore a soft smile that held many secrets. Damon didn't know how Angela had managed to find an artist who could so perfectly capture the spirit of his grandfather, but she had.

And in that moment she'd made him feel less alone. Popa would always be there with him.

The painting gave him the courage to go on. But lately it had lost its power.

"Tell me what's going on," Damon said.

Angela jumped up when she saw him.

Damon gently pushed her back down. "When's the last time you've eaten?"

"It doesn't matter."

He sat down beside her. "It does. You look worn out. Let me—"

Angela shook her head. "I don't have time and I didn't plan to stay long. Just give me a yes or no. Can I work for you? After I get your answer, I have to go back to the hospital."

"Hospital? Who's sick?"

"My son—"

"What's his name?"

"Doesn't matter," she said impatient. "He's sick and could die because of me."

Damon pulled out his cell phone. "I doubt that. Which hospital?"

She gave him the name.

He frowned. "Can he be transferred? I know of another one that—"

"I don't even want to consider it. This is the best I can do and I still don't have the money for the medicine he'll need to clear his infection let alone the hospital stay and—"

He put his cell phone away. "Consider it done."

"But I haven't told you everything yet. He'll also need--"

Angela abruptly stopped when Vanessa came into the room with a plate of fruit and cheese. She thanked her then waited to continue after the other woman left the room.

"He'll need surg—"

Damon cut her off. "He'll get everything he needs. Trust me."

Relief replaced the desperation in her eyes. She hesitated before she said, "I'm glad you found someone." She bit her lip. "Are you still..."

"Dying?" He nodded, picking up a pear slice. "Yes."

"I'm sorry."

He bit into the pear. "Me too. And she's not my fiancée either."

"Oh." She chewed her lip. "Do you still want one?"

"A wife?"

She nodded.

Damon sighed. "I'll take care of your son, you don't have to—"

"I know, but it doesn't seem fair for you not to get anything out of it. Unless you've changed your mind about wanting a wife."

He should say he had. He should say that he'd moved on and accepted that his life would soon end. He should say that he didn't need her. But she was here and he didn't want to let her go. As foolish as that was.

His mother was still pestering him about Vanessa. He sent Angela a considering look. "What if I have changed my mind?"

She held his gaze. "I told you, I'm willing to do *anything*."

He took a deep breath. Those words had more of effect on him than he wanted them to. "We'll see." He picked up a pear slice and held it out to her.

She took it unsure. "What is this?"

"People usually eat it." He stood. "And you need your strength."

"My strength?"

"Yes. Take a couple more with you. Now let's go."

To his relief she popped the fruit in her mouth before she grabbed another one. "Where?"

"The hospital." He noticed her take a cubed cheese before he said, "I'll be right back." He hurried into the kitchen and saw Vanessa leaning against the counter with her arms folded. "What's going on?"

He pushed her aside to open a cupboard. "I need a container to put the fruit and cheese in so Angela can take them with her."

"That's not what I mean."

"She needs my help and I'm going to help her. We're going to the hospital." He pulled out a glass container and closed the cupboard. "Thanks for the food."

Vanessa grabbed his arm before he could leave and said in an urgent voice, "Are you sure you can manage this?"

He felt a flash of anger and briefly regretted telling her the truth about his illness. This was the kind of worry he hated. He couldn't let his diagnosis stand in his way. He had to be strong for Angela. For her son. They both needed him. He took a deep breath, taking hold of his temper and reminded himself that Vanessa wasn't the enemy, she cared about him. "I'll be fine. I don't know how long I'll be there so you'd better go home."

"Call me when you get back."

"I will." He kissed her on the cheek. "Thanks."

"You've already said that. When you call, tell me who she really is."

"Remember to lock up." He darted out of the kitchen before she could say anything more. He returned to the living room ready to gather up the fruit and cheese, but stopped when he saw the mostly empty serving plate.

Angela shrugged at his stunned expression. "I was hungry."

"Ravenous more like it." He set the glass container down. "I guess we don't need this. Let's go." He walked out the front door and pointed to his BMW. "I'm driving. Get in."

"But what about my car?"

"No one will steal it."

"I mean—"

"I know what you mean, you'll get it later. Right now I'm driving you to the hospital. Do you want to know why? Because you look like you haven't slept in a few days and I don't feel safe being driven by a woman like that. It's nothing personal."

He also needed something to do with his hands because if he didn't, he was bound to wrap his arms around her and hold her tight.

CHAPTER FIFTEEN

Jadin was going to get the treatment he needed. That should have eased Angela's anxiety but it only seemed to escalate.

She felt as if she were seeing Damon again after many years instead of only months. And with a touch of guilt she wondered how a man who was dying could still look so good. Was it right for a sick man to still have such beautiful brown skin? Should the color of his eyebrows and eyelashes still be so black? Should his shoulders still be so broad and remind her of the time he'd held her when she'd thought her life was falling apart?

Angela took a deep breath, feeling her body grow warm. Damon hadn't gotten married, but that had to be because he didn't want to. There were plenty of women who would enjoy being the woman by his side let alone in his bed.

"Is she your girlfriend?" Angela asked although she was annoyed with herself for being curious.

"She's a friend."

There was something he wasn't telling her. They seemed

to be closer than just casual friends. What would she think of his crazy scheme and why hadn't he asked the other woman to marry him?

"So what's his name?" Damon asked.

Angela cleared her throat. "Is this a new car?"

"No, and why do you keep avoiding the question?"

She paused before she reluctantly said, "His name is Jadin."

The car swerved. Damon got it back under control before he turned to her stunned. "Why that name?"

Angela sighed. She could understand his surprise and confusion. It was the name he'd given one of the projects they had worked on together.

"It has to have a name," he'd said. They had been sitting in her office with a winter rain pounding against the window, but the room felt hot with excitement and ambition. Both his and hers.

Angela drummed her nails on the desk. "Why?"

"Because it's our first official project together. We're parents and this is our baby. We'll call it Jadin. I had a childhood friend called that and he was always lucky. What do you say?"

"I think it's silly."

"You don't like the name? Fine, I can think of something else."

Angela waved her hand surprised by such a sentimental streak. "Never mind. The name is fine."

Damon slapped the desk, pleased. "Good, we'll both make sure Jadin is a success." And it had been. He'd name other projects Samantha, Keisha, Kenji but they'd always teased each other about their first born as a private joke.

Angela glanced out the window annoyed that the memory

of those projects still brought her a feeling of joy. They had had good times together. "I don't know. Perhaps it reminded me of better times. I didn't mean to."

"Then why did you do it? I thought you hated me."

She looked at him. "I don't hate you."

"But you did."

"It was more complicated than that."

"But—"

"I liked the name and it was a memory of a good time, okay? Plus, I may not like you but I thought it was sad you were getting cut off in your prime. I plan to call him by his middle name anyway," she lied.

"Which is?"

"Sotero."

He swerved again.

She glared at him. "Stop doing that."

He pounded the steering wheel. "Then stop surprising me."

"Why is it a surprise?"

"Because Sotero's *my* middle name!"

"No, it's not."

He glared at her. "You know it is. You saw it when you helped me on one of my book tours. You made fun of it, remember?"

Yes, she did. She still remembered the embarrassment on his face when she'd discovered it. She'd learned he'd given himself the first name Damon, like his grandfather, at seven years old, to his mother's horror. For months she refused to call him by that name, determined to refer to him by his birth name of William, until Damon wore her down by refusing to respond to her otherwise.

He'd then, briefly, shared that his grandfather had given

his middle name to him (his father loved it, while his mother didn't) and then she remembered telling him her middle name and him telling her how beautiful it was and then... "Oh, right. I must have kept it in my subconscious."

He sighed.

He had a right to sigh. She couldn't tell him the truth. That ever since she'd met him again, he'd been on her mind; especially the night she'd gone into labor. Even when she'd been alone in the room after her mother and sister had gone, she'd thought of him. Wishing they'd managed to have stayed friends so she wouldn't feel so alone.

"At least he doesn't have your last name," she said.

Damon paused. "Would you like him to?"

More than anything, Angela wanted to tell him. She wanted her son to finally be safe. He'd be safe as Damon's son.

But it was too much. "If you adopt him he'd—"

"Have access to my estate when I die? I thought of that. You'd also be well provided for as my widow."

"I'd rather not think that far."

His face hardened. "It's not as far away as you think. I'm a man living on borrowed time."

"You don't have to leave the estate to him. You have family. But I am willing to marry you. Just tell me the terms of the arrangement and what I have to do."

"We'll discuss that later. Right now we'll focus on Jadin."

CHAPTER SIXTEEN

"You didn't call," those were the first words Vanessa told Damon when he emerged from sleep and answered the phone at four in the morning.

He yawned. "What?"

"I told you to call me when you got back. I've been waiting all this time."

"You could have waited until tomorrow."

"*Tomorrow* was two days ago!"

He ran a tired hand down his face. "Oh." He wasn't surprised. He'd lost track of time. He wasn't a big fan of doctors and hospitals, although they'd become a part of his life. He barely registered what the doctor said only hearing that Jadin needed care as soon as possible. He told them to do whatever was necessary. After that everything seemed to have happened so fast.

The doctor was able to get Jadin into surgery early the next morning, Angela kissed her baby's forehead before they whisked him away. She didn't cry although he could tell she wanted to.

Together they waited.

And waited.

He'd never been so anxious for anything in his life. And that's one thing he ended up silently bargaining. He bargained his life, his wealth, anything in exchange that Jadin be okay and that the fear in Angela's face be swept away.

The doctor returned with a smile and told them the surgery had gone well and Jadin would soon be in recovery.

Angela was so relieved she let him hug her. Or perhaps she'd hugged him. He wasn't quite sure. All he remembered was the joy and relief he felt holding her in his arms. A dark chasm had been crossed and they'd survived it.

"Damon, are you awake?" Vanessa demanded.

"Unfortunately." He rubbed his eyes. "You could have called me."

"I did call. I left messages. Texts. I even stopped by but you weren't home."

"Sorry about that."

"Then tell me what happened."

"Everything is fine."

"That's not what I asked," Vanessa said. "Who is she?"

"I guess you should be the first to know. She's going to be my wife. Now go to sleep." He disconnected at her sound of surprise and turned the phone off.

But he wasn't able to go back to sleep.

Angela had agreed to marry him.

He'd twice given her an out. Told her that he'd help her son no matter what but she felt a marriage of convenience was a fair exchange and he didn't plan to argue with her.

He wouldn't spend his last holiday alone.

He'd already told his house manager and the rest of the

staff to prepare for her arrival. He'd given them special instructions for Jadin's nursery and told them to spare no expense with Angela's bedroom.

Angela didn't love him. She barely liked him, but she was still what he needed.

The past several months since he'd last seen her had been consumed by tests, medicines and doctor visits. He worked but with little enthusiasm, just enough to fool those around him, but not enough to fool himself.

Not enough to remove the emptiness that had haunted him since he'd last seen her that cold day in late October. He'd cut his work and travel schedule, reducing the number of interviews and guest appearances, giving vague excuses as to the reason. He told his brother he wanted to focus on other aspects of the business—property holdings, licensure deals, and investments to make sure they were all solid. He told himself it was to preserve his health, he knew it was because he didn't care as much as he used to.

But now he did care.

He had a goal and purpose. Something to believe in.

Now he had a chance for redemption. He could make up for his past mistakes.

He planned to treat her the way she deserved to be treated.

He planned to treat her like a queen.

CHAPTER SEVENTEEN

A thief.

Or at least a potential one. That's what Angela had been branded in the eyes of the shopkeeper who was keeping his gaze on her. The barrel-chested Mr. Kim, who had twice followed her around the store trying, but failing, to inconspicuously track her.

She couldn't blame him. On top of job losses and foreclosures, shoplifting was on the rise. She understood business. She knew that losing thousands of dollars a day could destroy a business. But understanding didn't make his distrust of her any less painful. Especially when she was standing in the same aisle with an attractive young woman who had already tucked baby formula, diapers and tuna into her baby's stroller.

This man didn't have any eyes on her. Even though her brunette hair was in need of a wash and her clothes looked worn. It didn't matter that Angela had entered the store in her best pressed jeans and blue shirt. That she'd entered without a large bag (in which to hide items in) or a baby stroller (same) since her baby boy was still in the hospital. It didn't matter that she was picking up tissues because she'd spent the last couple of days crying. She wasn't an ordinary customer.

She was the potential threat...the other woman wasn't.

The woman tucked a toy into the stroller. Then their eyes met.

Startled hazel eyes clashed with a knowing brown gaze.

The woman's expression quickly shifted from shock before it looked frightened. Then pleading. Pleading for Angela to understand and not say anything. Angela understood that desperation too. For the past several months she'd done everything she could to make sure her baby was okay. She'd had to scrimp and scrape—squeezing a nickel until it screamed—in order to make it through each day. Even the meager items in her cart had been carefully budgeted.

But she wouldn't be rewarded for that conscientious effort. It was expected, but this woman was stealing...and getting away with it.

Angela turned away and headed for the counter. She wouldn't report her.

She offered a forced smile to the clerk, even a nod to Mr. Kim whose wispy black hair and large reading glasses hanging around his neck, reminded her of the father of a friend she'd had in school. His father had famously publicly scolded him when he broke his arm after doing a dangerous stunt on his bicycle (he'd lied and said he was studying at a friend's house—hers. She later got an earful from her mother with Megan gleefully laughing in the background). But the memory of his father's comic outrage—they both swore his father's face turned the color of a pomegranate— made Angela smile and helped to humanize the shopkeeper. It was better than being angry. "You have a great selection of items here," she said.

"Thank you," he said. She saw his shoulders relax. She

sensed some trust but not fully. He gruffly gestured to a row of fruit cups and beef jerky displayed on the counter. "These are on sale."

The same young woman bought a stick of gum and potato chips. The clerk and Mr. Kim smiled at her and asked the age of her baby. He came from around the counter and with a kind grin headed to the baby's stroller. Angela sensed the woman stiffen, if he got too close he would see the strange bulge in the back.

"Oh, wait," Angela said. "Where are your paper towels?" Mr. Kim turned to her and showed her while Angela complimented him on how well organized everything was and he proudly shared how long he'd been in business. She asked him some pointed questions about the posters in his window highlighting store sales and motioned to the three foot high stack of boxes, left in the corner, which she assumed to be slow moving items. She made some marketing suggestions, which he was surprisingly receptive to and eager to learn more. So a minute diversion ended up becoming a nearly twenty minute conversation about the recession, the retail market and how best to serve customers.

Angela left the store no longer worried about the thief or that she'd spent more than she'd planned to. Helping the shopkeeper with ideas had felt good. It was what she loved to do.

She opened the trunk of her car, the late May sun beating down on her as if it had forgotten summer was still a few weeks away, and put her purchases inside.

Her life was changing today. She was picking up Jadin from the hospital and then she was moving into Damon's house. She'd called and let him know when they should be there.

It was her only choice. She couldn't imagine returning

Jadin to the dank basement apartment. But it meant facing Damon and realizing how much he'd rescued them. How grateful she'd been when he stayed, waiting with her all through Jadin's surgery. How he'd allayed her fears. How his steady, calm gaze gave her the strength she needed to make it through.

It pricked her pride how much she'd had to depend on him. But for the sake of Jadin, there was no room for pride.

"Thanks for not saying anything," a female voice said behind her.

Angela spun around startled.

The thief hadn't fled with her bounty. Instead she was looking at Angela with tears of gratitude spilling down her cheeks.

CHAPTER EIGHTEEN

Angela had briefly forgotten about her and was surprised she was still there. She shrugged. She really didn't want to talk.

"It's my first time."

Angela nodded, knowing the young woman's words were a lie. The woman was too calm and practiced for it to be her first time.

"I lost my job," she continued in a rush, "and I'm not producing enough milk so I need the formula but it's kinda pricey you know? And—"

"It's okay, you don't have to explain." Although Angela knew she wanted to. She didn't want to hear it. She had her own problems. But the woman wanted her to see her as more than a thief. Angela could understand that. Just as Angela had wanted the storekeeper to see her as more than a potential one. She'd wanted him to know that she used to be a professional woman with a great job and apartment. That this life she was living now wasn't who she was.

She felt herself softening towards the woman. They were both new moms trying to make the best of a hard time.

"Do you need a ride?" she asked her.

"You wouldn't mind? I was going to take the bus."

"It's fine."

During the drive, Angela learned the woman's name was Becky and her daughter's name was Emily. Her boyfriend split about three months ago when they both lost their jobs at a construction company and the stress of bills and a baby had driven them apart. Angela told her about the DRCA and others like it but Becky wasn't interested. She was optimistic she'd find work soon.

Optimism was good.

Angela turned down one of the residential streets Becky had directed her to and glanced at one of the single-family homes with boarded up windows. A few houses down she spotted another brick-faced house with the family's belongings —a large bed frame, an armoire, a couch—scattered in the front yard. She saw a little boy of about six holding a teddy bear while three adults gathered up what they could.

She quickly shifted her gaze forward, her heart aching. Foreclosures and evictions had unfortunately become a common sight.

She wasn't the only one facing broken dreams. But not everyone was.

While this family was struggling to pull their life together her sister was planning a trip to Hawaii and getting her kitchen redone. Again. Life was a funny thing.

She heard Becky sigh. "I envy you. Must be nice to be rich."

Angela turned to her alarmed. "What makes you think I'm rich?"

"This car for one. It's a Mercedes SUV and smells fresh off the lot. Plus you wear designer clothes and have the jewelry to match."

Angela was tempted to tell her that her car may smell new but it had a lot of miles on it. That she wore designer clothes because, even after losing her job, she knew the best consignment stores and she had a number of outfits she'd managed to still fit from her former high profile life.

But she didn't tell Becky any of those things. Instead she thought about her words: Must be nice to be rich.

She nodded and said, "Yes," knowing that in a week or two she'd marry Damon Reemer.

Then she wouldn't just look rich, she truly would be.

CHAPTER NINETEEN

But she feared the man she was about to marry was a little delusional.

That feeling of dread swept over her that evening the moment she walked into the nursery Damon had created for Jadin.

After picking her son up from the hospital, she'd arrived at Damon's house with all her worldly possessions packed in her car and walked into a room that could have fit her car and three others without touching.

Angela looked around the nursery in mild horror, holding Jadin close to her almost afraid to set him down anywhere in the luxurious room. "It's too big and—beautiful," she quickly added when she saw a flash of pain and disappointment in Damon's brown eyes. She'd seen that look before, whenever someone said a careless biting remark about his food or his business. She'd forgotten how intense he could be. That was why he hadn't done as well on television at first. While the camera loved him it also revealed every expression on his face.

On cooking-challenge shows he made contestants nervous by how much he studied them.

Even those he allowed to try his food felt as if they were under the microscope. Demon Damon was a nickname he had yet to get rid of. And yet he couldn't help but care what others thought as much as he pretended not to.

Relief quickly replaced the brief hurt in his gaze and he clasped his hands behind his back, satisfied. "I tried to think of everything, but let me know if there's anything more you want."

More? What more could someone want? It really was too much.

"Come," he said with eagerness. "Let me show you your room."

She was a little less horrified but no less impressed. He had outdone himself and made a spare room into a luxury suite. Bedding decorated with a fanciful, swirling pattern that complemented the chandelier of dangling crystal prisms above a large wooden bed.

"Again, if you need any changes—"

"It's fine," she said quickly. "Perfect. Thank you."

"I thought I'd let you settle in for a couple days before I formally introduce you to the staff. Okay?"

She nodded. "Do they know?" she asked, hating to mention his illness.

He shook his head. "Only you and Vanessa." He turned.

"Wait. One more thing."

He looked at her curious. "Yes?"

"You haven't really told me what to do."

He frowned. "Do?"

"Yes. I know you want me to keep your secret and marry you, but you must want more than that."

"You're right," he said in a deep tone, his dark eyes capturing hers. "I do."

Her heart began to race. She swallowed but boldly held his gaze. She'd come too close to back away now. "What?"

"Pretend that you love me."

CHAPTER TWENTY

"Always?"

"No," Damon said sounding amused. "Only when someone is around. Especially someone from my family." He paused. "Think you can manage that?"

Right now she was so relieved and grateful that he'd saved her son's life and taken her out of the basement apartment that she could kiss him senseless. She turned to look at her son no longer able to hold Damon's piercing gaze. "I said I was willing to do anything."

"Just making sure," he said.

Angela cleared her throat and looked at him uncertain. "How will we explain separate bedrooms to them or your staff?"

He stared at her with a blank expression. "What's there to explain? My parents always had separate bedrooms."

"Oh."

He turned. "I'll get your bags."

"Are you sure you can manage?"

He spun around. A flash of anger heated his gaze. "Of

course I can manage," he said in a voice so cold it made her shiver inside. "I can also manage to dress myself and feed myself too."

"I was just making sure. I'm sorry."

"I don't need you to worry about me. I've got Vanessa for that. All I need from you is to play a role. A simple role. Nothing else. Understood?"

"Yes," she said in a tight voice.

Damon marched out of the room.

Angela released a long breath. This was the Damon she remembered. Hard. Changeable. The one who had cut her out of his life when he'd no longer needed her. She'd been foolish to offer him even the slightest show of compassion. A man like him didn't need it. He just wanted people to do what he paid them to.

She was no different than the staff he'd talked about. There was nothing more to their relationship than that. She'd never mention his illness again, she wouldn't care. She'd only pretend to love him.

Which would be one of the greatest challenges of her life.

He hadn't meant to snap at her.

Damon hit the railing as he headed down the stairs. Everything had been going so well until he lost his temper. But he couldn't stand the thought of her pitying him.

He'd been eager to see her response to the nursery and he hadn't been disappointed. She'd been impressed. She'd liked the bedroom he'd chosen for her too. In her eyes he'd been a rescuer, a provider.

He felt like her hero.

And then she'd turned him into an invalid.

He'd promised her that she'd never see him if things got bad. Why wouldn't she believe him? He didn't need a nurse. A caretaker. She needed to understand that.

He grabbed her car keys from where she'd placed them in the hall, went outside and opened the trunk of her SUV.

He wasn't dead yet. He was very much alive.

So alive that not only was his blood simmering with regret and humiliation but lust.

He wished, just once, she'd look at him with the same hunger he felt when he looked at her. He had to force himself not to stare at her full lips, the gentle curve of her breasts hidden under her blue shirt, the sensuous shape of her hips, which her jeans only emphasized. He wanted her to wrap her body around his so that he could show her, in no uncertain terms, how very much alive he was.

To feel her warm breath against his neck, feel her tremble in his arms when he whispered her name.

He pulled out a large suitcase and let it hit the ground with a thud. Damn. It was heavier than he'd thought. He took a deep breath. He could have his staff empty her SUV later, but he couldn't back down now. If she could stack up her car, he could empty it.

He slowly took the first suitcase up the stair wishing he'd installed an elevator and set it against the wall in her room.

Angela sat on the bed, holding Jadin who found the button of her shirt fascinating and kept pulling it. He met her watchful, superior gaze. She didn't think he could make it. He would prove to her that he could. He turned and left.

By the time he'd carried the sixth suitcase—each one feeling as heavy as a two ton boulder—sweat plastered his shirt to his body and he was breathing hard enough to make his lungs hurt, but he couldn't stop. He had two more items to get. He couldn't show any weakness. He swallowed and put the bag down and flexed his hand, hoping his shoulder and forearm wouldn't spasm.

"That's enough," Angela said in a cutting tone.

He wiped sweat from his eye. "I'm almost done."

"You're finished now."

Damon glared at her. He'd come this far and she was going to argue with him? "I've got two more-"

"No, you don't."

When he turned to walk out the room he felt something soft hit the back of his head. He looked down and saw it was one of the pillows from her bed. He lifted it up amused and waved it at her. "You really think this will stop me?"

Angela stood. "No." She walked over to him and pressed Jadin in his chest. "Hold him," she said and he was going to argue with her, but then she let go and there was no way he was dropping a baby. So he held Jadin close with both hands. He was sweaty but to his relief the baby didn't seem to mind, instead making a game of splashing his little palm against the stream of water on Damon's neck as if he were playing in a puddle.

"Where are you going?" he demanded when she walked past him and headed out the door.

"Stopping this."

He followed her down the stairs. "I told you I was almost done."

She mumbled something he couldn't hear before she reached the main floor and marched out the front door.

Damon swore then looked down at Jadin who was looking up at him. "Don't tell your mom I said that."

He walked outside surprised he hadn't noticed how chilly

the evening was. He was about to comment on wanting to get Jadin out of the cold but the loud thud of a trunk hood being slammed closed stopped him. He felt Jadin jerk in surprise, but to Damon's relief the baby didn't cry.

"I can't believe you emptied it out," she said.

Damon stared at Angela confused by her anger. "I said I would."

"All by yourself."

"Of course."

"And you almost emptied the interior too." She slammed the back door closed as well.

He covered Jadin's ear. "Stop doing that. You're scaring him." But that wasn't true. The baby didn't seem particularly bothered. It was Damon who felt on edge.

Angela faced him with her hands on her hips. "And you're a stubborn idiot."

"Look, I'm sorry I snapped at you. I—"

"You have nothing to prove." She pointed to the SUV. "I had *four* people help me load up my car and you nearly emptied it all by yourself?"

He looked at her stunned. "You had help?"

"Yes. Serena, her husband and her nephew and niece. She'd given me some stuff she didn't need anymore, that's how I ended up with this many bags. So you don't have to prove how strong you are. You already have." She disappeared inside the front seat then reemerged with a bottle of water. She took off the cap and held it out to him. "Drink."

He was in no mood to argue with her. He took the bottle and guzzled down the water like a man emerging from a desert.

"Thanks."

She snatched the bottle from him. "Let's get a few things straight."

He cleared his throat, hoping his teeth wouldn't start to chatter. When did the evening get so cold? "Can we go inside first?"

"In a minute."

He looked down at the baby who was gazing up at the stars. "I think Jadin's cold."

"Jadin's fine."

Damon shivered from both the chill in the air and the ice in her tone. The woman was evil. "Okay."

"I may have to pretend to love you, but I won't pretend not to worry. You may be dying but I won't let you kill yourself."

"I wasn't—"

"Go inside and change before you freeze to death on a beautiful spring evening." She flashed a cold grin. "If you die now, I won't get to be a wealthy widow."

He didn't feel cold any more. He felt hot. Boiling hot. But not from anger. From triumph. This woman could match him. He needn't have been afraid that his temper could scare her away.

She was the right woman for him.

He held Jadin out to her and laughed. "You're right. I'll be more careful next time."

She took Jadin from him and nodded. "Good."

He pulled off his shirt and wiped the sweat from his forehead. "Now we understand each other."

"Yes."

He walked up to her and dropped his shirt on her head. She screamed in outrage and ripped it off and threw it at him. "That's disgusting."

He walked inside. "It's payback."

She followed him and closed the door. "For what?"

"You could have told me the truth after the third suitcase. Letting me carry six is just mean."

"I was making a point."

"Your mother is a sadist, Jadin."

"And your father is a masochist."

Damon paused, surprised by how nice and natural those words sounded to him. Your father. Yes, he'd soon be Jadin's adopted father. And Angela would be his wife.

The thought made him happier more than he wanted to admit and he wished he could kiss her and truly make her his.

Instead he gave a tiny bow in concession before he winked. "Then I guess we're well matched."

CHAPTER TWENTY-ONE

*L*usting after a dying man was just wrong. Angela sat in a plush grey chair in Jadin's nursery as her son slept. But she couldn't do the same. Every time she closed her eyes she pictured Damon stripping-um...taking—his shirt off.

Revealing a delicious column of chocolaty brown skin and muscles that moved with tantalizing motion almost begging to be touched.

Being angry at him was easy.

Frustrated, annoyed, infuriated even a little concerned was okay.

But attracted? Aroused?

No, that was just wrong on so many levels. It didn't matter that he was still so beautifully made. The moonlight and the porch light seemed to be competing to see which one could highlight his form better in the soft touch of the evening. Both gently pushed away the dark shadows that surrounded him like a sculptor cutting away wood to expose the form underneath.

But it hadn't only been his body that had captured her interest. It was his tenderness with Jadin. He held her son with such tender care—at times cupping his cheek, sweeping his hand over the baby's head, patting his back—it was annoyingly sexy.

Angela took a deep breath.

No, she wouldn't be swayed. It was a moment of weakness. It was because she'd been worried about him. *That* was what had heightened her awareness of him. It was her concern that made her watch the broad expanse of his back, it was her concern that made her notice a small river of sweat travel down his neck and disappear under his shirt.

The man was foolishly stubborn. Her job was to pretend to love him, not want to jump his bones.

She didn't know when she eventually fell asleep, but when she woke up she felt the weight of a blanket. She hadn't felt so renewed in a long time. She looked in on Jadin, pleased that he was still—amazingly!—asleep, which gave her enough time to brush her teeth, change her clothes and unpack some things before she had to take care of him.

Once he was fed and changed she headed for the kitchen her stomach growling.

It growled even more when the scent of buttered raisin bread, scrambled eggs and roasted peppers wafted out the kitchen.

The tropical décor didn't surprise her. The eat in kitchen with beige flooring and a farm house sink, with white cabinets that reached to the ceiling almost made her think that if she looked out the windows she'd see palm trees and the Caribbean Sea.

"Something smells delicious," she said, expecting to see Damon at the stove.

But he wasn't there. Instead she saw the tall figure of another man with his midnight black hair pulled back into a ponytail at the base of his neck. A crisp white collar peeked out from under a navy blue suit. He had skin the color of sun kissed dates and a chiseled jaw.

"Breakfast is ready," he said placing a plate of food on the kitchen island.

"Are you the chef?"

"No." He held out his hands. "May I?"

Angela stared at him, her mind suddenly going blank. She didn't quite know what he was asking for until he nodded towards Jadin and gestured forward. She mechanically handed him her baby, getting the sense he was the kind of man who was used to having people do as he said. She watched the man place Jadin in a baby seat she hadn't noticed before.

"Reemer is out," he said.

"Okay," Angela said, annoyed that she felt disappointed. She was looking forward to seeing him, which didn't make sense since she'd seen him last night. She scooped up the eggs and took a bite of the toast. "This is delicious."

"I'll tell the chef you're pleased."

"Who are you?"

"I'm to look after you. I am the house manager and will make sure that everything runs smoothly. Call me Tonto."

Angela nearly choked on her eggs. She set her fork down and laughed. "And Damon's the Lone Ranger?"

The man didn't laugh. "I don't know what you mean. Who is this Ranger?"

Angela's amusement fled. Shame and embarrassment made her cheeks burn. "Tonto is really your name?"

"Yes, it has a long history in my family. I've never heard someone laugh at it before."

To make fun of a proud indigenous man's heritage was terrible. She glanced down and saw the red maple leaf logo on his belt. "Canadian?"

He nodded.

"I-I'm sorry. I wasn't laughing at it. I thought you were joking."

"Why would I joke about my name?"

She waved her words away. "Never mind."

"I noticed you didn't sleep in your room. Is there anything wrong with it?"

"No, no it's perfect."

"Once you've finished breakfast I'll introduce you to the rest of the staff."

"Staff?"

"Yes, for a house this size we're rather small. There's the housekeeper, Reemer's personal assistant, chef and the groundskeeper. But any issue please address to me first."

"Yes, of course."

Minutes later, after Tonto had given her a somber tour of every level of the house, Angela came to a stunning conclusion.

She might have to pretend to be in love with Damon, but she was hopelessly in love with his house: From the landscaped garden, pool and stone patio to the large windows welcoming sunlight in the family room. When she put Jadin down for a nap and snuck one for herself in her new bedroom, Angela moaned in pleasure at the feel of the soft sheets against her skin.

And the silence was heavenly. She didn't have to try to fall asleep to the sound of a sump pump or Serena's TV blaring above her.

She later indulged in the luxurious waterfall shower and enjoyed a sumptuous lunch of grilled chicken and yellow rice.

Damon's staff suited his house perfectly from his smiley faced housekeeper, grim faced personal assistant (who didn't feel Damon used him enough), studious chef and wiry groundskeeper who proudly told her he was stronger than he looked. They all welcomed her and answered any questions she asked them.

Not that she had many questions. She had entered Paradise.

CHAPTER TWENTY-TWO

"I met Tonto," she told Damon that evening as they ate dinner—braised scallops over spiced brown rice in the kitchen. He hadn't told her what had kept him from home all day and she didn't ask. She assumed it was work related. She was just pleased that he'd invited her to join him.

Damon set his glass down. "Who?"

"Tonto. Your house manager."

Damon looked at her amused. "Oh...him."

Angela narrowed her eyes as a slow realization came to her. "His name isn't really Tonto, is it?"

Damon's mouth trembled with suppressed laughter.

"It's not funny."

He nodded, his eyes dancing with humor. "Yes, it is."

"You should pretend to fire him just for the fun of it."

"Fire who?" a familiar voice said, coming into the room.

Angela pointed at him. "Why did you trick me?"

He shrugged as he handed Damon a clipboard and pen. "Just following orders."

She looked at Damon. "You told him to do that?"

Damon quickly signed what his manager had given him before returning the clipboard and pen to him. "I really didn't think you'd believe it."

"Are you still upset about the suitcases, little Sambo?" she said, referring to the controversial hero of a series of children's stories.

Damon rested a hand on his chest and widened his eyes in mock horror. "Would I be that petty?"

"Good evening," The Man Not Named Tonto said before he started to leave.

"No," Angela said. "Sit down. You're not leaving until we clear up a few things."

The man looked at Damon for assurance. He nodded.

She pointed at the two men. "See? That's going to have to stop. I don't want private looks shared between you."

The Man Not Named Tonto sent Damon a secretive look. "Did you hear that? No more private looks."

Damon formed his lips into a pout. "I'll miss those."

"I'm serious," Angela said.

"I can't believe you're giving me up for her," The Man Not Named Tonto said with a sigh.

"It can't be helped," Damon said. "She loves me so much, I felt a little sorry for her. How could I say no when she basically begged me to marry her?" He shifted his gaze to hers. "Isn't that, right?"

Angela opened her mouth then closed it knowing she couldn't say what she wanted to with an audience. What was worse was that he knew it and was enjoying himself. She saw the laughter and challenge in his eyes.

"Right," she said through gritted teeth.

The Man Not Named Tonto sensed the sudden tension in the air and stood. "I should go."

"Sit down," Angela said using the tone she'd once used with a difficult client. "And if you look at him one more time for assurance I swear I will get my revenge."

The man sat.

"Thank you. What is your name?"

"Ray."

"Are you really from Canada?"

He nodded then stood. "Good evening."

"Wait, I haven't finished talking to you." Angela stared open mouthed as Ray calmly walked out of the room. She turned to Damon who was finishing his rice. "Are you going to let him treat me like that?"

"Relax. It's nothing personal. He treats *me* like that. He's a very busy man and he makes sure I have few things to worry about so I have no complaints. Besides, you're lucky you got him to stay as long as you did. He must like you."

Angela sent him a dark look. "At least I don't have to pretend to love *him*."

"Yes," Damon said with a chuckle. "Lucky you." He glanced at his watch before he pulled a quarter out of his pocket and placed it on the table. "So who should go first?"

Angela frowned at him confused. "First?"

"Heads you tell your family we're getting married. Tails I do."

"We have to tell them eventually, what does it matter when?"

"I bet my family acts stranger than yours."

Angela sniffed. "You haven't met my sister Megan."

"You're on." He pulled out his cell phone. "Call her and put it on speaker."

Angela sighed. "You can be such a child."

He folded his arms with a smirk. "Small pleasures."

She dialed.

The phone rang.

And rang.

Angela's mood began to brighten with hope. "She may not be home."

Damon rested his chin in his hand, his expression amused. "I can wait."

On the fourth ring her sister picked up.

"Hello?" Megan said.

Angela's mood plummeted but she forced a light note in her voice. "Hi, Megan. It's me."

"What's wrong now?"

"Why would anything be wrong?"

"Because that's the only reason why you call me. So what is it?"

Angela sent Damon a look. "I just have something to tell you."

"You'd better not be taking Ronald back."

"I'm not. Why would I do that?"

"Because you're desperate."

"That's not true," Angela said outraged. "I—"

"Oh, so it's perfectly normal for a woman to lie to her mother and tell her she's still with an ex-fiancé who's abandoned her?"

"I'm sparing her feelings. Something that's a foreign concept to you."

"You're living in a place that smells like the sea."

Angela rubbed her forehead. Calling her sister had been a bad idea. "You don't know that."

"You told me it was a little dank I can imagine the rest and you're—"

"I'm getting married," Angela quickly said to cut her sister off from saying anymore. "Megan?" she said when the line went silent.

"Hmm."

"Did you hear what I said? I'm getting married."

When silence followed her words, Angela said, "Megan, are you still there?"

"Yes and I heard what you said. Both times. I just didn't want to believe it. Again, I realize you're desperate—"

"I'm not desperate."

"But marrying the first man who comes along is—"

"I've known him a while."

"Who?"

Angela looked at the man sitting across from her. He lifted a brow in question, challenging her to tell the truth.

"I'm marrying Damon Reemer."

Her sister fell silent again before she said in a tight voice, "That's a really sick joke."

"I'm not joking."

"You really expect me to believe you'd married the man who completely destroyed your career?"

Angela sent Damon a nervous smile, her face burning. "Wait, now he didn't—"

"His one action destroyed your reputation and toppled all that you built so of course when they restructured the business and jobs had to be cut you were one of the first to go. Then that other job Ronald got you went bust. On top of that—"

Angela reached for the phone to take it off speaker, but Damon grabbed it before she could.

"People started to doubt whether you made him or he made you," Megan continued. "He went on with his life and yours went down the drain. You could even partly blame him for Ronald."

Angela reached out her hand to Damon and mouthed, "Give me the phone."

Damon slowly blinked and shook his head.

"You two fought about a lot of things," Megan said, "but mostly about all the time you devoted to the demon. Remember that was the nickname you gave him?"

"I didn't give him that nickname. He already—"

"Anyway, I never told you this but Ronald once thought you were having an affair."

"That's because Ronald's an idiot," Angela said through gritted teeth then mouthed to Damon, "But he's not the only one."

He looked back at her unfazed.

"What was that?" Megan said. "You sound far away."

Damon bought the phone a little closer to Angela, but grabbed her wrist to stop her from taking it. "I really need to go."

"Not until you tell me why you really called."

Angela tried to yank her wrist free, Damon calmly kept his hold. "I just did."

"You're seriously thinking of marrying this guy?"

"Yes."

"Why?"

She looked at Damon. "Because...I realized I was wrong about him and—" Angela briefly closed her eyes as she said the words she was expected to say, "I love him."

"No you don't," Megan said in a flat voice.

Damon pointed to phone and mouthed, "Try harder."

Angela cleared her throat. "Yes, I do. He's—" She stared at him searching for inspiration. "He's not bad looking and he can cook."

Damon stared at her stunned and mouthed, "That's it?"

She shrugged. "And he's great with Jadin. That means a lot to me."

Damon looked oddly pleased by the compliment, which made Angela notice how good looking he really was and wonder why he smiled so rarely. Something she didn't want to think about.

"I see," Megan said. She fell quiet for a moment before she said, "So it's not because he has a lot of money and you need it?"

"No, absolutely not. Oh...Damn, Jadin's crying. I have to go. Bye," Angela said then used her free hand and sunk her nails into Damon's arm, causing him to drop the phone so she could disconnect.

"You are a rat," she said.

He rubbed his arm. "I know." He paused. "I'm sorry."

"For being a rat?"

"No," he said in a quiet voice. "I didn't realize I hurt you as much as I did. If I'd known—"

She shrugged. Her face still burned from humiliation. "I'm glad you didn't. I wouldn't want you to work with me out of pity and we both realized you didn't need me."

"That's not why I—"

"At least the worst is over," Angela cut in. She didn't want to talk about the past. "I'm sure telling my family beats telling yours."

A cold smile touched his lips. "Just wait and see."

CHAPTER TWENTY-THREE

*L*eo picked up after the first ring. "It's about time. You know Vanessa called me and told me—"

"That I'm getting married?" Damon said.

"No. That you'd disappeared for about two days. She was worried." He paused. "Wait. You're getting *what*?"

"Married."

"Well, it's about time. Vanessa is great."

"I'm not marrying Vanessa."

"Why not?"

"Because I'm marrying Angela Watkins instead."

His brother swore.

"I'd prefer congratulations."

"That's impossible."

"To say congratulations?"

"To think about marrying that woman. Do you still feel guilty?"

Damon sent Angela a look. "A little."

"Why? This could ruin your life. She's the worst woman for you. How did this even happen? No. Don't tell me. I bet she came up with this scheme, didn't she? You'll do anything she says, just like you did back then. I know you regretted what you did, even told me you didn't mean it, but it was for the best. I got you out from her grasp. The same woman who told me she made you and could destroy you."

Angela stared at Damon wide eyed and mouthed, "I never said that."

Damon rubbed his chin, his face expressionless. "What else did she say?"

"That you're pathetic. Remember when you couldn't get a hold of her and you asked me to contact her instead?"

"I do."

"That's when I found out what she really thought of you. That she thought your best opinions came out of her mouth."

Angela jumped out of her seat. "That's not—"

Damon held up his hand and stopped her.

She glared at him and mouthed, "But I never said those things."

He glared back and mouthed, "Keep your mouth shut."

"What was that?" Leo asked. "Is someone with you?"

"Sorry, I was playing music. I turned it off." He sent Angela a quelling look and motioned to her seat.

She folded her arms and sat.

"And you're going right back to her," Leo said finishing a thought neither of them had been listening to.

"Think Mom will be pleased?"

"Sure, once she wakes up from a coma. You don't know what you've done. Have you listened to anything I've said?"

"Yes."

"And you haven't changed your mind?"

"I have."

"Really?"

"Yes, I don't think you'll make the best witness at our wedding. Talk to you later." Damon disconnected at his brother's sound of outrage.

"So," Damon said, putting the phone on mute when it rang again. "Who had it worse?"

Angela narrowed her eyes and leaned forward, resting her arms on the table. "You clever bastard."

He nodded. "Thank you."

She ignored the sarcasm in his voice. "You didn't do this phone call competition to compare whose family would react the worst. You wanted me to find out what really happened all those years ago."

He shrugged. "You wouldn't listen to me, I thought hearing it from Leo would be better."

She pointed to the phone. "But he lied. I never said those things to him."

Damon shook his head. "Leo doesn't lie."

"So you're saying I do?"

"No, maybe in the heat of anger you forgot what you'd said."

"I didn't say those words."

"Perhaps there was a misunderstanding."

"I didn't say anything remotely like that." She held out her hand for the phone. "Let me talk to him."

Damon moved the phone out of reach. "You can do that later." He tucked the phone away and leaned back. "I'm sorry things ended the way they did. I was too proud to make things right between us."

Before Angela could reply, her cell phone rang. She looked down at the number and said, "I have to take this," before she left the room.

In the hallway she answered the call and said, "What?"

"I need to see you," Megan said. "Serena told me you moved out."

"You called Serena?"

"I was hoping she could talk some sense into you. Where are you?"

Angela cupped the phone and said in an exaggerated whisper, "In hiding from my nosy sister."

"I need to see you. Otherwise I tell Mum—"

"I'm at Damon's place."

"Give me the address."

"We can meet at a—"

"Now."

"I swear if you ruin this for me and he kicks us out, I'll never forgive you."

"Why would he do that? Doesn't he want to marry you?"

Angela hesitated. "Yes, but—"

"And I thought you were in love with him."

"I am but—"

"Then he'd better get used to you having visitors."

Angela relented and gave her sister the address and set the time. She returned to the kitchen and sat down with a heavy heart.

"My sister is coming over Saturday," she told Damon who was also tucking his cell phone away.

"So is mine. Don't worry. We'll be married before then."

Angela looked at him surprised not because of how soon they'd get married but because she'd learned something about him she'd never known. "You have a sister?"

"Yes."

"You never mentioned her before."

"There's not much to say. Once you've met Leo you've basically met Helen."

CHAPTER TWENTY-FOUR

*W*hich was not exactly true. While Helen did have the same coloring and conservative dress as her brother, her energy was more tightly wound. Her body hummed like a windup toy as she sat facing Damon and Angela in the family room. She hadn't touched any of the assortment of tiny fruit tarts laid out for her on the coffee table.

"This is highly irregular."

Angela also learned that Damon's sister tended to use phrases that didn't quite make sense.

"And why are you dressed like that?" she asked motioning to Damon's chef jacket.

"I told you I came back from a photo shoot and didn't have a chance to change."

"You look ridiculous sitting there like that. You look like you work instead of live here."

"Do you want to meet your nephew?" Damon said, sounding bored, as if he'd grown used to her insults. "He's napping, but if you're quiet—"

She bristled. "No."

"Then why did you come?"

"I had to see this travesty for myself."

"What makes it a travesty?"

Helen bristled again as if bees had crawled up her blouse. "Marrying a stranger—"

"Angela is hardly that."

"Nobody knows who she is."

"You mean the *right* people don't know who she is," Damon clarified.

Angela raised her hand. "And in case you haven't noticed I'm sitting right here."

"Mom is in such a state," Helen said ignoring her. "It's an egregious joke."

"It's not a joke."

"You're right. Jokes are supposed to be funny but this is ..." Her words fell away.

"A travesty?"

She nodded. "Exactly. Why would you think of marrying a woman with a baby?"

Angela waved her hand. "Still here."

"I care about her," Damon said, turning to Angela, his dark eyes smoldering with heat she didn't expect to see. He took her hand in his, his voice deepening, "And she cares about me." He held her gaze and Angela fought to hold it afraid her body would burst into flames. She'd never had a man look at her like that and especially not Damon. He turned back to his sister. "Trust me, our feelings for each other took us both by surprise."

Angela leaned slightly forward and released a deep breath shocked by how good an actor he was. He squeezed her hand in warning not to let her guard down so she quickly gathered herself and faced his sister who was looking at them with suspicion.

"Why the rush?" Helen said.

"Mom wanted me to get married, so I did," Damon said sounding confused. "Some women are hard to please."

The doorbell rang. Angela jumped to her feet eager to escape. "That's probably Megan."

They continued to ignore her. But when she took a step forward she realized she couldn't move.

Damon still held her hand. He wasn't letting go on purpose.

Angela turned to him and said in an overly bright voice, "Honey, I need to get the door."

"No, you don't. Someone else can get it."

She narrowed her eyes in warning. "But I told you I was expecting a guest and would like to welcome them."

He stared at her for a long moment before he released her.

"Excuse me," she said to Helen before she dashed to the front door. "I've got it!" she called out to Ray who was heading towards it. She pushed past him and opened the door.

To her shock her sister was grinning. It was a scary grin. An evil grin.

"You clever girl," Megan said.

"Stop looking at me like that."

She stepped inside. "I completely understand now. This gorgeous house alone is worth the inconvenience of a husband."

Angela closed the door. "I'd hardly call him an inconvenience."

"At first I thought you were crazy. But you have sense after all. I've changed my mind. Marrying for money is one of the oldest and most lucrative career moves a woman can make."

Angela glanced over her shoulder. "Keep your voice down."

"Are you afraid he'll hear us? I doubt our voices would carry past the foyer. Which is beautiful by the way." Megan nudged Angela in the arm then began slowly walking around the room. "Good girl."

"I didn't marry him for his money," she said relieved that such a blatant lie didn't choke her. "I told you. I love him."

Megan stopped walking and shot her a look. "I was there when you created an effigy with his face."

"I was mad at the time."

She walked up to the large bouquet of flowers and took a sniff. "And the dart board."

"Feelings change."

"I'm not here to judge." Megan paused in front of an ornate mirror and fixed her hair before she continued her circular excursion around the foyer. "No, that's a lie. I'm here to say good job. I know why you married him, but what reason did he give you?" She gave her sister the once over taking in Angela's simple black trousers and grey blouse. "It's not your sex appeal."

Angela rested her hands on her hips. "Well, thanks a lot."

"Darling, I love you, but there's no use lying. You've never been fashionable. You've been professional, but that's it. And now you've got at least fifteen pounds of baby weight—"

"Hey!"

Megan bent forward to study a wooden figurine holding a spatula. She turned it slightly. "But it doesn't matter. You were unemployed and broke. Now you're wearing a ring that could feed and house a hundred families for an entire month, you're living in this gorgeous house and don't have to work another day."

Angela moved the figurine back. "Who says I don't have to work?"

Megan's brows shot up. "He's forcing you to work?"

"He's not forcing me to do anything. I want to work."

"Why? This is your chance to be a woman of leisure. Volunteer, join a board, shop and get a hobby."

"I have nothing against those things, I just want to do something else."

Megan glanced up at the high ceiling. "How was the ceremony you didn't invite me to?"

"Don't take it personally, it was a rush."

"A formality you mean," Megan said unfazed. "I know there was nothing romantic about it so I didn't miss anything."

Angela folded her arms, annoyed by how right her sister was. Their wedding was as romantic as a twenty minute business meeting.

"I wore white."

Megan looked at her amused. "Did he notice?"

No, which made Angela feel foolish for going through the hassle of buying the simple white dress and matching shoes. Damon didn't look at her with any interest. She didn't realize that one of the most important days of her life would be so unmemorable. But it didn't matter. She'd gotten what she'd wanted out of it. "He was very complimentary," she lied.

"Sure. Where's my nephew anyway?"

"Sleeping in the nursery," Angela said drawing out the last word hoping her sister would be impressed.

Megan flashed another evil grin. "I promise to be quiet."

CHAPTER TWENTY-FIVE

The nursery managed to do one thing Angela had never been able to do. It left her sister speechless.

Megan slowly walked around the large room in awe almost leaving the room without looking at her nephew before she remembered why she'd entered the room in the first place.

Megan remained speechless as Angela led her downstairs but when they reached the main floor and Ray passed them offering her a brief nod of greeting, she regained the use of her tongue.

"Who is that?" Megan asked, looking at him with sharp curiosity before he disappeared into another room.

"He works for Damon," Angela said in no mood to expand. She wanted to get the visit over as quickly as possible. "I'll introduce you later," she said, planning to conveniently forget. She led her sister to the family room. However, she abruptly halted when she spotted Damon's sister, Helen, still sitting there humming with indignation.

She took a hasty step back. She didn't want Megan to meet Helen just yet. "Let's go somewhere else."

"Why not there? I told you I wanted a tour. Unless you want to introduce me to that guy who works for Damon instead..."

Angela heard whirring in the kitchen. "Yes, let me start with the kitchen." She walked in and found Damon standing at the counter blending something. He had his back to them.

Megan's evil grin widened as she walked towards the kitchen island. "And the house comes with a chef." Her gaze traveled the length of him. "A sexy one at that."

"Lower your voice."

"Does he take requests?"

Damon grabbed two glasses giving them his profile.

"He looks familiar," Megan said. "Where have I seen him before?"

"He's not the chef," Angela said.

"But he's dressed like—"

"He's a chef, not *the* chef."

"He's been on TV, right?"

Damon set one of the glasses filled with a strawberry colored mixture in front of Megan and flashed his practiced smile. "Among other places."

She whimpered and held out her hand. "I'm Megan."

Angela stared at her sister stunned. It wasn't like Megan to melt at the sight of a man but she'd become putty within seconds of meeting Damon. She cautiously studied her sister wondering what game she was up to.

He shook her hand. "Damon."

"The same name as her husband."

"That's because I am."

Megan rested a hand on her chest. "Wait, you're *him?*"

Angela nudged her sister in the side. "I told you he was."

"But he doesn't look anything like the dartboard. It must be the lack of a goatee and devil horns."

"I look different in real life," Damon said.

"Better." She laughed. "Especially without your eyes gouged out."

Angela waved a dismissive hand. "She doesn't know what she's talking about."

Megan turned to her. "Yes, I do. That—" Angela sent her sister such a dark look Megan had the grace to look ashamed and quickly said, "uh...thing that didn't happen."

Damon flashed a grin that Angela knew he used to get his way. "Mind if I borrow your sister a minute?" he asked her.

"Sure," Megan said sounding willing to give him anything.

Damon pulled Angela aside and lowered his voice. "Seems to be going well."

"Well enough. Right now I'm sweating blood."

"Your sister seems nice."

"'Seems' being the operative word. Right now she's applauding me for being a gold-digger and simpering over you for—" They both turned to Megan who was sipping the drink Damon had given her. She caught them looking and waved her fingers at them in a coy manner. Angela turned away and shivered. "Heaven knows why she's acting this way."

Damon rubbed the back of his neck. "Better than being a sucker. I can't seem to get Helen to leave."

"Do you want to swap siblings? I think we could both use a reprieve."

He looked at her with hope. "Think that will work?"

"No harm in trying."

"Ten minutes then I'll come and rescue you." Damon handed her the second glass. "Good luck."

CHAPTER TWENTY-SIX

*H*elen took the drink Angela offered her with all the joy of someone receiving poison before she said in a tart tone, "Where is Damon?"

"He's talking to my sister right now," Angela said taking a seat in front of her. "He'll be back soon but wanted me to give you this."

She took a sip to Angela's surprise. She wasn't sure Helen would drink it. Perhaps Damon's sister just looked miserable. "My brother's libations are always refreshing."

Angela nodded wondering how such a conservative looking woman could make a word like 'libation' sound indecent.

"So was it love at first sight?"

Angela laughed surprised by the question. "Hardly."

"So it was the money then?"

"Yes, absolutely," Angela said hoping that teasing Helen might help her to loosen up. "There's nothing about your brother I find remotely attractive except for his money," she said making sure to be her most sarcastic. "I mean it's not because he's good looking, he's passable but not amazing. I don't care about his success in his career, the books, the shows, the restaurants. Even his apprentice program is nothing if not another celebrity trying to do good for their ego, right? He's shallow and simple which is the perfect man for me."

Helen stared at her a long moment. Then she threw her drink at Angela covering her in crushed iced and pulverized strawberries. "You disgust me."

"Wait, I was joking."

"That my brother is shallow and simple?"

"I meant the complete opposite of everything I said. Of course he isn't."

"I don't believe you. I believe you told me exactly how you feel. Our mother will hear about this."

"Please don't go."

But it was too late. Helen had already stormed out of the room. She heard the front door slam.

Angela wiped her eyes and sighed before she walked into the kitchen.

Megan and Damon stared at her in shock.

"What happened?" Megan asked. "Sounded like something exploded."

"That would be the front door," Angela said. She shifted her gaze to Damon. "Well, I managed to get Helen to leave after she threw her drink at me and called me disgusting."

Damon blinked. "What did you do?"

"I made a small joke."

Megan nodded. "That explains it. You're terrible at jokes."

Angela motioned to her soiled clothes. "Not this bad. I said some things but I was being sarcastic. She didn't catch on at all."

Damon stood up and frowned. "I'm sorry. I forgot to warn you. Helen doesn't have a sense of humor."

Angela's brows shot up. "No kidding."

"What did you say?" Megan asked.

"Does it matter?"

"Sure. I could use a giggle. Although the sight of you is quite funny."

"Go home."

"You'll have to change and wash your hair."

"Now."

Megan turned to Damon. "See you again soon."

Angela glared at her. "Soon, as in next year, right?"

Megan grinned and wiggled her fingers in the coy way Angela was beginning to hate. "Bye." She left the room.

Damon studied Angela his face unreadable, but she sensed some amusement. "You're sister's wrong," he said. "You don't have to wash all your hair. Just the front."

Angela narrowed her eyes and pointed at him. "I swear if you crack even the tiniest smile, I will strangle you."

He blinked. "I wouldn't dare," he said before his lips spread into a wide grin.

She lunged at him. He laughed and darted out of the room.

"You are a sadist," Angela called after him.

"I thought I was a masochist."

"I changed my mind."

"I told you I forgot," Damon said with laughter in his voice.

"I should have left you with her."

He jumped over the couch. "At least you got her to leave." He looked at the area rug. "That stain's going to be hard to clean."

Angela growled and lunged at him again. He jumped out

of reach and raced down the hall. "I'm sorry, I'll make it up to you."

"Not unless you're willing to let me throw a hive filled with honeybees at your head."

"That's a little extreme."

"You sided with my sister!"

"Your sister scares me," he said.

"Your sister scares me more."

"Fair enough." Damon stopped running and held out his hands. "Oh, is that what you're upset about?"

"No, why should I be upset about anything? It's perfectly okay that your sister throws her drink at me and then you explain the reason for it without standing up for me."

He furrowed his brow. "Is that your attempt at sarcasm?"

She growled and ran at him again.

He ran into the kitchen again. Then spun around and stopped, waving his hands. "Wait. Okay." He took a deep breath. "I can't outrun you. You win. Tell me what I did wrong."

Angela released a sigh in frustration. "You really don't know?"

He shook his head.

"You're supposed to be my husband, right?"

He nodded.

"And yet not once did you ask me if I was okay, you didn't ask if she hurt me. You didn't try to comfort me. You didn't even offer me a hug."

Damon looked down at his clean shirt and then her stained one. "I'll give you a hug after you change."

"That's not the point. You didn't care. You don't care and I know that. I accept that, but at least try to *pretend* that you do care in front of others. Especially when it's my family."

He grabbed her hand and pulled her to him. "I'm sorry. Really. I didn't think about it like that."

She tried to wiggle free. "Let go. It's too late now."

"You're all sticky," he said holding her tight, then she felt something warm and wet against her cheek. "But not bad."

Angela took a step back and stared at him stunned. "Did you just *lick* my cheek?"

Damon licked his lower lip. "I hate to see such a good smoothie go to waste."

She touched her cheek. "I can't believe you just licked me."

His voice deepened. "Is it the first time a man's licked you?" He shook his head before she could respond. "No need to reply I think I know the answer."

"I'm not into licking."

"Why not? It's fun." He shoved his hands in his pockets and rocked on his heels. "Especially with the right toppings."

"Everything is about food with you."

He shook his head. "No, not everything."

His voice held too much promise. She wasn't falling for that. "I'm going to shower and change." She turned.

"Did she hurt you?" All humor had left his voice.

Angela turned and rolled her eyes trying to display a nonchalance she suddenly didn't feel. "It's too late now. Why do you care?"

His gaze held hers. "I do care."

She waved her hand in dismissal. "Never mind. It's over now. She's going to report me to your mother."

His brows shot up in alarm. "She's going to talk to my mom?"

Angela grinned, pleased by the slight panic in his voice. "Absolutely."

CHAPTER TWENTY-SEVEN

He had touched her cheek with his tongue.

His *tongue.*

He had put his wet, warm tongue and pressed it against her skin.

She should have been disgusted, insulted, horrified. Instead she wanted more.

More playfulness. More fun. More of him.

He'd done something unexpectedly sweet and sexy.

She'd been so distracted she didn't get a chance to find out what he and her sister had been discussing. She wasn't sure she wanted to. Her sister didn't know much about tact, but Damon didn't look insulted so whatever they were talking about couldn't have been that bad.

Angela placed her hand against her cheek. She could still feel the pressure of his tongue, feel the warmth of his body against hers. She didn't want to think about it. To think about the brief way he looked at her, not with teasing but with warmth. *I do care,* he'd said.

She sniffed. As if she'd fall for that.

Unfortunately, her still racing heart seemed to. It was because it was a trying day that was all. She didn't care if he cared. They were both getting something out of this strange arrangement.

But for the first time she looked at him and felt heartbroken. She hadn't felt this heartbroken before. She'd felt sorry for him, a little sad. But never heartbroken. But a part of her felt a loss. He wouldn't always be here. She wouldn't always get a chance to be annoyed or angry at him.

But if he hadn't been dying she wouldn't be in his life. It was meant to be. At least he looked well. He didn't seem to be in too much pain or in any pain at all. She was afraid to ask him. She knew how much he hated talking about his illness and she wasn't sure how much he wanted her to know so she kept her distance.

If he wanted to tell her more she'd listen, but she wouldn't push him.

She could see why he hadn't told his family though. With a sister like that his last few months would truly be a torment. Helen would regiment everything, probably check his pulse every two minutes, and have someone by his bedside and check to make sure he was breathing.

No, this had been the right choice.

Angela took a quick shower then went to check on Jadin. He wasn't there. Her first instinct was to panic then she realized it was unlikely he'd crawled out of the crib himself.

Finding him ended up being easy. She just had to follow the sound of high pitched giggles.

She found Jadin and Damon in the family room sitting on

the ground. Jadin with two pillows positioned against his back to keep him upright, clearly finding Damon's version of peek-a-boo the height of hilarity. She'd never gotten him to laugh like that before.

Damon scrambled to his feet when he saw her, his gaze unsure. "He woke up and you were still in the shower, but I didn't want to leave him there so I—"

"It's okay," she said. Her cell phone rang and she saw that it was her sister. She groaned. At least it wasn't her mother—yet. "I have to take this. Do you mind watching him for a couple more minutes?"

"Not at all."

He sat back down on the ground with an eagerness she hadn't expected, one that made her heart skip a beat. He truly liked her son. That meant a lot to her. He was different with Jadin, less guarded, more real. Even though he'd let her in on his secret she felt as if he kept her at a distance. That he kept everyone at a distance. What had made him stop trusting people?

But she couldn't care.

Angela left the room and answered her phone. "Don't tell me you left something here as an excuse to come back."

"Why would I need an excuse?" Megan said.

"Never mind. What was that crazy behavior?"

"I don't know what you're talking about."

"You were flirting with him."

"No, I was testing him. You don't see the way he looks at you. I was just curious to see what kind of man he is."

"That shouldn't be hard. He's a man who likes women."

"No, he's a man who loves you."

"What?"

"I know you say you love him, but...be careful. Don't hurt him."

Angela stood frozen not sure she could trust her hearing. "What are you talking about?"

"I've never met such a sad lonely man in my life. I really thought you were with him just for the money at first but now I see that there's more to it."

Angela couldn't believe what she was hearing. Were they talking about the same man? How could Damon be lonely? He was usually surrounded by people. But he did have a right to be sad. He didn't want anyone to know about his illness, but if he hadn't told her she wouldn't have suspected anything. How had Megan sensed it? She couldn't mention his secret but she could rebuttal the rest. "There's no danger of me breaking his heart."

Megan sighed. "You really are dense."

"What?"

"You can't tell that he's in love with you?"

Damon was a consummate actor. She didn't know how he'd managed to fool her sister so completely, but she'd have to play along. She knew he wanted her to pretend to love him but she hadn't expected him to pretend the same. "We love each other. That's why we got married."

"But he loves you more."

"That's not true."

"It's as clear as a centrifuge."

Angela rolled her eyes. "Why do you say things like that? It doesn't even make sense."

"Now you sound like Mum. Of course it makes sense. A centrifuge—"

"I don't care."

Megan fell silent for a moment then said, "I know Ronald

hurt you but don't take it out on this guy. He's one of the good ones."

"He slipped something in your drink, didn't he?" Angela said wanting to make light of her sister's words even though they shook her.

But her sister didn't respond. All she heard was the sound of a dial tone.

The man was amazing.

Angela stood in the hallway and watched Damon playing with Jadin as if he'd been the baby's father since the beginning. The adoption hadn't even become official yet. That would take a longer process than their marriage.

But the joy on Jadin's face and the devotion on Damon's let her know that a piece of paper was only a formality. A bond had already been set. Her baby had fallen for him as most people seemed to. It was no surprise Megan had believed whatever part of himself Damon had shown to her.

She walked into the family room trying to show a nonchalance she didn't feel. "You're really good. You actually got my sister to believe that—" She stopped. She didn't want to say the words aloud. The thought was ridiculous.

Damon looked up at her and blinked. "Got her to believe what?"

"Never mind. Want me to make something to eat?"

Damon turned to Jadin and said, "The thought of your mother in the kitchen makes me want to cry."

Angela gently nudged him in the ribs with her foot. "I can cook—sort of. I'm getting better."

"Don't bother. There's plenty of food in the kitchen."

"I like to cook sometimes."

"I'll never trust someone who can enjoy burnt cake."

"You still remember that?"

"It's seared in my brain," he said in a somber voice. "The nightmares still come."

"It really wasn't that bad."

"I rest my case." He glanced at his watch. "Besides, you don't have to worry about cooking. The chef should be here soon."

Damon rushed to his feet then stumbled forward, reaching out to the couch to steady himself, but missing it. She grabbed him to keep him from falling.

"I got you," she said in a gentle whisper, holding him tight, his solid back pressed against her chest.

His voice hardened. "I don't need—"

She held him tighter. "It's okay."

He didn't move. His body tense.

"I'm sorry I chased you."

"I can run," he said in a hoarse whisper that lingered on the edge of pain and shame.

"I know. Just not as much as you used to."

He hung his head.

"But you're still amazing so it doesn't matter if you need help. Rest against me."

He slowly shook his head.

"I won't let you fall." She paused considering the size and weight of him. "Or if I can't hold you, we'll fall together. Trust me."

"I always did," Damon said in a low voice. "I don't think

you ever knew how much. I think in your eyes I was just a client, a project, a way to a promotion."

"I never saw you like that. I wanted to see you succeed." She began to pull her arms away, but he stopped her, keeping her arms around his waist.

"And I did thanks to you."

She bit her lip, being this close to him she became aware of the faint scent of coconut oil that clung to his shirt, hear the slow, deep rhythm of his breathing, and felt the heat of his body that his clothes couldn't hide.

Demon Damon.

His nickname flashed in her mind and she wondered why he didn't frighten her. Why he never had. "It wasn't just me. You were the one with the talent."

He shook his head. "But it wasn't enough. You made me want to do more. You made me dream bigger than I ever thought possible." He took a deep breath and she could feel his whole body move. "I...I pushed you away because you meant too much to me. I depended on you too much. It scared me. It angered me if I'm being honest. I handled it wrong and I'm sorry."

"You don't need to apologize anymore," Angela said, unnerved by the sadness in his voice. *He's one of the loneliest men I've ever met,* Megan had said. And at that moment Angela believed her. In spite of all that he'd accomplished. The accolades, the women, the friendships, his family and a staff ready to cater to his every whim, at that moment he sounded like a lost boy aching for forgiveness and something more.

He pulled away from her. Angela stood, briefly shocked by how cold she suddenly felt without him. He sat down on the couch and held out his hand to Jadin and let the baby grab his finger. "Yes. I do, because I'm not being completely honest."

She sat facing him, wishing the cold feeling that had skittered over her skin would go away. Wondering why she had a strong urge to hold him once more. Except this time she didn't want his back to her, she wanted to face him as she did now.

She folded her arms, trying to take hold of her warring feelings. But Damon didn't look at her, instead he made a funny face at Jadin making the baby grin.

"Damon."

He picked up a soft rattle with the head of an elephant and gave it to Jadin to hold, shake or chew on, whichever he picked. "What?"

"That past is over. You don't have to think about it anymore."

"I envied Ronald."

Angela studied him not sure if he was teasing her or telling the truth. "Stop that."

"What?"

"Lying."

"I'm not lying. It's true. You took my breath away."

"I don't believe you. You can't even look at me."

"No. Because it hurts too much. Do you think it's easy admitting how much of a fool I was to let you go?"

"If this is your idea of a joke—"

"It's not," he said with a tired sigh. "Believe me. I'd never fallen for a woman so hard." He lifted his gaze. "I'm a dying man. Why would I lie?"

Now that he was looking at her, his dark chocolate brown eyes searching hers, she couldn't face him. She didn't want to face the feelings he could arouse in her. Feelings like longing and desire that she'd thought she'd put behind her. She glanced at Jadin who was chewing his fist. She didn't know what to think. How to feel. She'd been attracted to him too, but she could never have imagined that he'd felt the same. She held her arms tighter to her chest, feeling her temper flare. There was no use dredging up the past, it was too late to think of a future since they didn't have one. All that mattered was now. "I wish you'd stop saying that."

"What?" Damon said with amusement. "That I'm dying?"

Angela glanced out the window at a slow moving white cloud drifting across the deep blue sky. She didn't understand why he thought it was funny. She could find no humor in the thought of him dying no matter how light he made of it.

"Angela, look at me."

She chewed her lip, keeping her gaze on the lone cloud, wondering why it was the only one in the sky. She didn't want to look at him, but she knew she had to. She shifted her gaze to his face and had to fight not to look away again because his eyes held such tender compassion they nearly brought her to tears. He knew what she was thinking and didn't judge her for it.

"Ignoring it won't make it any less true," he said. He looked at her for a long moment, before he briefly closed his eyes and shook his head. "No, don't do that."

"What?"

He opened his eyes, his voice sad, "Feel sorry for me. This won't work between us if you do."

"I don't feel sorry for you," she said, determined to make him believe her. He'd given Jadin and her so much she didn't want to make him sad. She tilted her head and brightened her tone. If nothing else, she wanted to make him smile. "Why would I feel sorry for a gorgeous, successful, wealthy man who happens to have a wife like me in spite of all his flaws?"

Damon narrowed his eyes. "I can see why my sister threw her drink at you. Your sarcasm needs work."

"Have you never heard of a backwards compliment? What is wrong with your family?"

He lowered his gaze. "We don't hear compliments very often." He took a deep breath. "Have you ever had the feeling that your parents love you but don't like you very much?"

"No, my mother was too busy."

"Well, that describes the Branson family. We're always falling short somehow. All my life I've been trying to reach an imaginary bar and it's only recently that I've realized I don't think it exists. Never did."

"I'm sure—"

He raised his foot, stopping Jadin from trying to crawl underneath the couch. "Nope, don't try to tell me what I want to hear. I love my mother and she loves me, with limits. I've grown used to that." He bent down and took a piece of string Jadin had managed to find and took it before the baby put it in his mouth.

Angela stood and took the string from Damon and stuffed it in her pocket. "But you've achieved so much."

"I've never had a long-lasting relationship, I failed trig, I have a failing business, I never reached the financial level my father did at my age, I haven't—"

Angela picked Jadin up and sat down beside Damon. "When I first saw you I wanted you." She paused and adjusted Jadin on her lap. She delicately cleared her throat, feeling her face burn. "No, wait... that came out wrong."

A glint of humor lightened his eyes. "Actually I liked how that sounded."

She swallowed, wondering if it had been a bad idea to sit down next to him. He wasn't much taller than her, but he had an ability to take up space, to force you to be aware of him. And right now she was aware of every aspect of him, from the way his trousers fit snugly over his well sculpted thighs to the size of his hands, but she had to focus and ignore his teasing. "When I first saw you on the TV I saw something—someone— amazing. I knew you were someone I wanted to work with. I knew you were bound to do great things and I wasn't wrong. Look at you now, you've accomplished so much, but you haven't stayed still. You try new things. I like your spirit. You were always willing to do what I told you, I didn't need to convince you. Working with you had been so—"

"Would you work with me again?"

Angela stopped, unsure what had surprised her more: His question or the eagerness in his voice. "Again?"

"My illness may be a secret but one thing people will soon know about is how much the DRCA program is failing. I could use your help."

Sitting this close had been a mistake. Her heart wouldn't pound this fast if she'd been on the other side of the room, she wouldn't be so aware of his eagerness and feel it igniting her own. Her skin wouldn't tingle and she wouldn't feel herself coming alive with excitement.

Damon stroked the top of Jadin's head and said to him, "Tell your mommy I'm willing to beg if I have to."

He'd probably kept this information from Serena to protect her from the full extent of the program's status. But it was just the kind of project Angela needed so she wouldn't think about him. About what he was starting to mean to her. "You don't need to beg," she said. "I'll have you on your knees for another reason."

He met her gaze. "What's that?"

"I'll make the DRCA such a success, you'll worship me."

Damon lifted a mocking brow. "Those are bold words."

Angela stood, ready for a battle. And she had an advantage. She'd been part of the DRCA program and had noticed some of its weaknesses. She had an insider's view of what needed to be done. She'd had to prove herself before and she'd do it again. "They aren't just words. They're a declaration."

CHAPTER TWENTY-NINE

The wrath of Jeannie Branson was both swift and expected.

Damon had been waiting for his mother's reaction to his marriage since his sister's visit.

So he wasn't surprised when his mother showed up on his doorstep, her temper as hot as the summer sun. She wordlessly stormed into the house. He opened his mouth to suggest they meet in the study but she headed to the family room before he could stop her. He inwardly swore. Angela was playing with Jadin there. His sister Helen had been an experience for Angela, he didn't want her to have to deal with his mother so soon.

"Mom. I think—"

She spun around and slapped him.

Hard.

"I don't care what you think after the stunt you just pulled."

"It wasn't a stunt."

She bristled with indignation with not a hair out of place.

She wore dark trousers freshly pressed and a red silk blouse free of the slightest crease. "Do you enjoy humiliating me?"

"How did I humiliate you?"

"Marrying some stranger no one knows about!"

She turned and stopped when she saw Angela on the floor with Jadin. She walked over Angela, as if she were a piece of litter placed in her way, and took a seat. "I'd like something to drink."

Damon started to turn to head to the kitchen. "I'll be right back."

"There's no need," his mother said. She gestured towards Angela. "The nanny's right here." She cast a negligent look in her direction. "You don't mind, do you, dear? And please take the baby with you."

"She's not—," Damon said at the same time Angela said, "I'm not—"

"Nothing with ice please," his mother cut in as if neither had spoken.

Damon sighed. "She's not the nanny. She's my wife."

Jeannie gave Angela a cool look before she said in a tone dripping with disdain, "Of course she is."

Angela rose to her feet and picked up Jadin. "I would say it's a pleasure to meet you, but my mother taught me not to lie."

"It's a shame she didn't teach you how to dress," Jeannie mumbled.

Angela opened her mouth to reply but his mother said, "If you will excuse us, this is a private matter."

"Nothing is private in this house. *My* house."

Jeannie turned her gaze to Damon, effectively dismissing Angela and said, "I will not forgive you for this. You humiliated me. Do you know how awful it felt talking to Vanessa's mother? We both had such plans. Your wedding was going to be—"

Damon shook his head. "I never said I'd marry Vanessa."

"Oh no," Angela said, facing his mother. "No, I'm not doing this again. Not like your daughter. You're not going to ignore me."

His mother sighed, pinching the bridge of her nose. "Tell her to leave."

Damon placed a hand on Angela's shoulder. "No."

His mother glared at him and folded her arms. "I'm not saying another word until that women leaves."

"*That* woman is not going anywhere," Angela said then placed Jadin on his mother's lap. His mother stiffened as if she'd just been handed a sack of potatoes. She'd never carried a sack of any kind in her life and didn't know what to do. Damon moved forward to rescue her, but Angela blocked his path and gazed at him with concern in her eyes, lightly touching his still stinging cheek. Her fingers gentle as a mist against his skin.

"Are you okay?"

Damon stifled a laugh. He knew she was supposed to pretend that she loved him but worrying about a simple slap was going a bit far. Plus, if he didn't find it funny he might forget and really think that the deep shadow of concern in her brown gaze was real. So real that for one wild moment he wanted to kiss her. "I'm fine," he said before he mouthed, "Don't overdo it."

He shifted his gaze and saw his mother awkwardly placing Jadin next to her. But he noticed she'd placed the baby too near the edge of the couch. Damon began to walk forward, but Angela placed her hand on his chest, stopping him.

Damon stared at her alarmed, the warm feel of her palm almost burning his chest and mouthed, "He could fall."

"He won't."

His pulse quickened when he saw Jadin start to tilt forward, but before he could somersault over the edge, his mother pulled him back and placed him in the corner. But Jadin wouldn't stay still and when he moved to the edge again she placed him on the ground.

"Take Jadin and leave me with her," Angela told him in a low voice.

He began to shake his head, but she surprised him with a kiss and whispered against his lips, "If you can trust me with your apprenticeship program, you can trust me with your mother."

He took a deep breath. He needed to take a deep breath because suddenly he was finding it a little hard to breath. She'd kissed him. It had been a light fleeting kiss, but it had lingered on his lips longer than the sting of his mother's slap. Her kiss left his mouth burning for more. Her kiss made him suddenly aware of her—the scent of baby oil, the yellow stain on her grey sweatshirt, the feel of her hand pressed against his chest. As if she was protecting him. But he didn't need protection. He didn't need her to stand up to his mother for his sake. Those were battles he was used to handling alone. But she was his wife. The contract may be real, but everything else about their relationship wasn't.

It was all pretend. He flexed his hand wishing he didn't want it to be otherwise. "She's not as easy to manage."

Angela narrowed her eyes. "I like a challenge." She leaned forward, briefly engulfing him in the scent of cocoa butter, and pressed a warm, sweet kiss on his lips before she whispered, "Now go."

"Okay," he said in a gruff voice, determined not to show

how much her playacting had affected him. He picked Jadin up and headed to the hall.

"Where are you going?" his mother demanded.

"He's giving us privacy," Angela told her. "I have a few things I need to say..."

Damon could only imagine what Angela had to say as her voice faded behind him while he took Jadin into the relative calm of his study. He always took comfort in the dark wood floors and grey walls, the custom built cabinets and desk with stainless steel countertop. He stood in front of the unlit fireplace. Part of him felt as if he was abandoning her but she'd asked him to leave and he had to leave or he might forget himself and kiss her back.

But although he knew staying away was the right strategy, that didn't stop him from worrying.

He paced the study, jostling the baby in a way that made him giggle with delight, and tried to think of what he should do next. How long should he stay away?

Angela might be strong, but she was no match for his mother. However, if he said he trusted her he had to show it.

But that didn't mean he couldn't spy.

He stopped pacing and cradled Jadin in one arm while he pulled out his cell phone and called Ray.

"I'm busy," Ray answered.

"You're always busy."

"I'm talking to the groundskeeper right now about a—"

"I need you to do me a favor."

"You don't pay me enough to do favors."

"I need you to see how things are going in the family room."

"They're fine."

Damon paused, surprised by his swift response. "You haven't even checked."

"I was told to tell you that everything is fine."

Damon switched Jadin to his other arm when the baby tried to reach for his phone. "Who told you that?"

"Who else? Your wife."

"When did she say that?"

"I was told that whenever your mother came I was to say quote everything was fine unquote. Bye." He disconnected.

Damon put the phone down on the desk then held Jadin out in front of him and said in wonder, "Your mother knew all along."

Jadin blinked.

Damon sat down on a sofa, placing Jadin on his lap.

She had been prepared for this moment. She'd planned to talk to his mother alone. He should have known. Of course she hadn't taken his sister's threat as cavalierly as she'd seemed to. She'd promised to help him with his family and she'd meant it.

But it had always been like that with her. She'd always been a few steps ahead of him. That's why he'd been able to succeed so quickly with her help. She knew what one action could lead to and how best to utilize every opportunity.

That's what she used to call challenges. She saw every challenge as an opportunity: When he'd lost the chance for an interview spot because the producer already had 'their black chef' Angela hadn't skipped a beat and landed him on two popular shows as a special guest. When his cookbook idea initially was rejected for being at once 'too ethnic' and then 'not ethnic enough' she'd found a small publisher willing to take a gamble and once the book was published helped make it such a success that both he and the publisher benefited both financially and professionally.

"I was worried for no reason," he said to no one in particular, feeling a lot less tired than he had a few moments before. She was in his corner. It felt good to have someone on his side like that again.

But nearly twenty minutes later Damon started to worry again. Conversations with his mother never lasted this long. Usually ten minutes the most. Within ten minutes she did her customary critique of his life, told him how best to fix it then left.

Twenty minutes was a rarity he couldn't fathom. What could they possibly be talking about?

He cracked the door open and listened. He didn't hear raised voices. Not that he expected that. The women in his family didn't shout. But he couldn't hear *anything*. Not a mummer, not a grumble. Nothing.

Unable to hide his curiosity any longer he left the study and stood outside the family room, hoping Jadin would stay silent so as not to give them away. But when he looked at Jadin he realized he didn't have to worry. The baby had fallen asleep.

He inched closer.

Still nothing.

Not a sound. Damon carefully peeked his head around the corner and saw his mother sitting there by herself.

"It's about time," she said. "I'd wondered when your curiosity would get the best of you."

Damon looked around the room. "Where's Angela?"

"She's not packing her things if that's what you're afraid of."

"I'm not."

A cool smile touched her lips. "If that were true, how come you're holding that baby like I'm a monster about to eat it?"

Damon relaxed his hold on Jadin. "What did you two talk about?"

"She'll have to tell you."

"Angela and Jadin mean a lot to me. If you hurt her—"

"I doubt a steel beam could hurt that woman. She's stronger than she looks. I see why you chose her."

Jeannie slowly rose to her feet, looking at him in a way he'd never seen before. She looked almost...proud. "I underestimated you." She touched his cheek. "I'm sorry. I shouldn't have struck you. I had my reasons but there is no excuse for that."

"I-it's okay," he stammered not sure he could trust his ears. His mother had never asked for forgiveness before.

She looked at Jadin then returned her gaze to him and said words he'd hungered for years to hear her say, "You did well," before she walked out of the room.

CHAPTER THIRTY

She felt as if she'd run a marathon.

Angela sat on the balcony and looked down at the gleaming waters of the pool below. She wanted to take a swim to cool off but felt so exhausted that she feared she'd drown instead. Just sitting up felt like an effort. She closed her eyes, inhaled the fresh air warmed by the sun, and released a long, deep breath.

Of all the women in Damon's life his mother had to be the most formidable.

His friend Vanessa's beauty and intelligence had their own intimidating aura, but Angela didn't sense the other woman disliked her, just wasn't sure of her and made it known. She found it a little endearing that Vanessa cared about Damon so much and still vaguely wondered why he hadn't married her instead.

Then there was Helen. Humorless Helen was truly terrifying.

But Jeannie was in a category of her own. Not only did she possess Vanessa's beauty and intelligence and Helen's lack of humor she had an acid tongue. Angela could now understand why Damon rarely smiled. Growing up with a mother like that she was surprised he'd ever learned to laugh.

But today she also discovered something extraordinary.

Jeannie loved her son.

Angela heard the sliding glass doors open and turned to see Damon staring at her, breathing hard as if he'd been running.

"What did you say to her?"

Angela froze not sure what to do. She was too tired for another fight and wasn't sure she was in trouble or not. "I told her the truth."

His eyes flashed with anger as he closed the sliding door. "About me being sick?"

She stood shocked when she noticed that he was empty handed. "Where's Jadin?"

"He's asleep in the nursery." Damon slowly walked towards her, mutiny in his gaze. "Did you tell her?"

"No."

"Are you sure? Are you sure you didn't even hint at it by mistake?"

She rested her hands on her hips, determined not to step back although every primal instinct of survival told her to. "I absolutely did not tell her. Why would you think that?"

He stopped. "Because...because..."

"Sit down. You look pale. Did something happen?"

Damon let her lead him to a chair and sat down stunned. "It doesn't make sense. What did you say to her?"

"I said a lot of things. Why?"

His hand shook as he rested it on his chest, his voice filled with awe. "She said she was sorry that she hit me. She told me that I did well." He lowered his gaze and shook his head. "She's never said that to me before."

"It's about time."

He lifted his compelling brow gaze to hers. When he spoke his voice was heavy with emotion. "I don't know how to thank you."

Angela shifted from one foot to the other feeling both embarrassed and pleased. "I didn't do anything."

"You lied and made her believe that I was worthy—"

"I didn't have to lie and you are worthy. You deserve heaps of praise."

Damon shook his head in amazement. "I told you to pretend to love me, but I still don't know how you managed to make her see that. Admit it, you exaggerated a little. Not that I mind."

Angela cleared her throat, leaned back against the balcony railing and folded her arms because the look of awe on his face made her want to hug him. "You're right, I did exaggerate a little. Instead of merely telling her you saved my son's life I told her that you gripped him from the hands of death and rescued him from a life of abject poverty."

He lifted a brow, his face expressionless. "Is this your attempt at sarcasm again?"

"Wait, wait I'm just getting started. I also told her that you not only rescued me from the edge of a nervous breakdown but that you also managed to tame the beast of my sister and turn her into a pussy cat. And...What you're leaving already?"

"I'm not leaving," Damon said, walking up to her, his steady gaze remaining on her face. His voice held an odd note she'd never heard before. "I'm enjoying this. What else did you tell her?"

Angela felt a wave of apprehension. She glanced up at the

sky unable to hold his gaze anymore. She'd been teasing him, but she wasn't sure how far she should take it. "I told her that the first moment I met you I was inspired to be better because of how amazing you are. I told her how lucky I feel to be with you."

He stopped in front of her, resting his hands on the balcony railing on either side of her, trapping her in the circle of his arms. "And that was all an exaggeration?"

Angela glanced at the ground then his hand then his neck even his chin. Anywhere but his face.

She couldn't face him right now. She couldn't look into his eyes. Not when he was so close and her body was fully aware of every aspect of him. An intense feeling of desire coursed through her as she inhaled the scent of him—a mixture of cedar wood and an array of spices that made her head spin. It had been months since they'd been this close together. When he'd pulled her into his arms and held her close when she'd thought her world was falling apart.

But that seemed a distant memory now about two different people.

Her world wasn't falling apart. It wasn't a cold autumn day, with a stretch of bleak clouds overhead. Instead, the summer sun shimmered over the lush green grass, dancing its way like diamonds floating on the water of the pool. She felt embolden by the power and wealth that surrounded her. Her world had expanded beyond her wildest dreams.

Facing Jeannie hadn't only been a challenge it had been a test. A battle to prove that she belonged. Not only in this house but with this man—a man she'd defended not only because she had to but because she'd wanted to.

She didn't want to push him away, although her rational mind told her to. Her rational mind told her Damon was even more dangerous to her heart than he'd ever been in the past.

But her body didn't wish to heed that warning. It craved not only the intimacy of secrets—the one they were hiding from those closest to them—but the intimacy of the primal heat of two bodies coming together as one. It was a desire that frightened her because unlike everything else—the teasing, the sarcasm—the desire was real.

"Angela," Damon said, his voice barely a whisper.

She felt her pulse quicken, aware how the sound of her name on his lips sounded like an invitation. "Hmm?"

"Was that all an exaggeration?"

She forced a laugh ready to press down the feelings he aroused in her. Sarcasm was a great shield and barrier. Sarcasm kept her safe. "Of course. We both know that—" She paused sensing the tension between them shift from playfulness to something more. There was a tense waiting energy that surrounded him. An energy that could burn bright or go cold. He was as still as a night sky. She could feel the weight of this tenuous connection that had formed between them.

She was vulnerable to it, but so was he. She had a choice: she could either break this bond or shatter it. It terrified her a little as she raised her gaze to look into his eyes not certain what expression she'd find there. Would it be casual amusement or that inscrutable dark look she hadn't managed to decipher yet? She knew he was a man with other secrets he wasn't willing to share.

She met his dark gaze and said, "I meant every word."

He didn't move. He didn't blink. He pinned her with that piercing look that made people uncomfortable and for a moment she wondered if she'd made a mistake. She didn't see desire in his eyes or lust—just focused intensity.

He took a deep breath and stepped back and her heart shattered a little at his rejection. "Really?"

She nodded steeling herself against the misery of loss. She'd taken a gamble to get closer to him and had failed. She walked around him. "I guess I should check on Jadin."

"He's fine," Damon said as she opened the glass door. "But I'm not."

She froze. "What?" She turned to him, his back faced her. He stood as a dark, lonely silhouette against the sky.

"I don't want to claim more than you can give. But I want..." He hung his head. "This isn't easy for me to admit. But with you I want..."

Angela stared at him and remembered another time they'd been close. Only days ago she'd held him when he'd lost his balance. He'd told her how he'd felt about her.

He felt the most comfortable revealing his feelings when he wasn't facing at her.

She was beginning to understand him.

And herself.

She rushed in front of him and cupped his face in her hands. "I kissed you once. Now it's your turn to kiss me."

His voice deepened, his smoldering gaze falling to her mouth in a way that made her lips tingle. "I want to do more than kiss you."

She smiled, all apprehension leaving her. "Kissing is only the beginning."

"Then what are we waiting for?" he said before he covered her mouth in a sweet, slow, tender kiss.

CHAPTER THIRTY-ONE

The sight of the baby monitor surprised her. It was one of the last things Angela had expected to find in Damon's bedroom. It stood out, as noticeable as a lighthouse—white and gleaming in the seductive dark hues of his bedroom—and sat on the side table next to his bed. It was almost in the identical location of where she'd placed hers.

"Need help?" Damon said, stripping off his shirt.

Angela shook herself out of her shock and pulled off her sweatshirt. "No."

"Let me know if you do," he said with a wink before he turned his back to her. He used his body to block her from seeing what he was doing, but she heard something rattle and the mirror next to his closet reflected him quickly removing two medicine bottles from the top of his dresser and hiding them in a drawer.

It was not her place to ask how he was doing health wise even though she wanted to.

It was not her place to start counting down the months he

had left even though that was tempting too. She didn't want to think about losing him.

"Are you sure you don't need help?" Damon continued to tease her when she remained planted in place. His tone remained light, but his gaze had become unsure.

Angela gripped her sweatshirt in her hands. She didn't want to think about her father abandoning the family or Ronald leaving her. This was different. Damon wasn't gone yet. She had him now.

All that mattered was now.

This man.

This moment.

This chance to be with him.

She tossed her sweatshirt on the ground. "Actually I do." She walked over to him. "The zipper for this pair of jeans can be *so* tricky."

"I'm really good with zippers." Damon knelt down in front of her. "Let me see what I can do."

"Be careful."

He looked up at her. "I'm always careful," he said before he slowly lowered the zipper in a way that made the tiny teeth unlock in a sensuously soft z sound. When he was finished he rested his hands on her waist and shimmied her jeans down to the ground.

"You can get up now," she told him when he didn't move.

He sent her a look, his voice deep. "You sure you don't like me in this position?"

She frowned confused. "In case you haven't noticed the bed is over there."

"But you're right here." He pulled down her panties. "And that's all I need."

Before she could ask him what he meant, he bent forward and she felt his tongue on her center. She gasped in shocked pleasure and stumbled back.

"What are you doing?"

"Stay still and I'll show you."

"You can't do that while I'm standing up."

He narrowed his eyes. "You have no idea." He inched towards her. "What I can do. Besides, I love a challenge."

She held him off. "Not this one. Not yet." She sidled over to the bed and crawled under the covers. "Another time."

Damon slowly rose to his feet his heated gaze assessing her. "Promise?"

Angela nodded not trusting herself to speak.

He took off the remainder of his clothes and slid on a condom. "Because time isn't on my side." He got into the bed beside her. "And I don't like waiting too long."

She wrapped her arms around his neck, bringing his body close to hers. "You don't have to tell me that. I know you."

He shook his head. "No, I don't think you do," he said and when his mouth covered hers he silently pledge 'but you're about to find out.'

And she did in the most delicious way.

The kiss on the balcony may have been slow and tender but the man was not.

Damon wasn't a man who simmered; he was a man who burned. Fiery hot.

Scorching her with the touch of his hands, searing her body with his hot mouth, and letting it wander everywhere.

He may have trouble expressing his feelings, but he had no trouble displaying his lust.

She remembered once seeing him at the height of his

prowess in the kitchen of his flagship restaurant. He owned the space like a ruler reigning over his kingdom. There was no hesitation; every motion was quick, efficient and precise.

He was demanding, obsessive, almost possessed and the sight of it had both thrilled and terrified her. She'd never seen a man so passionate in his work and those around him watched in studied awe.

She never imagined he could be passionate about anything else until this moment.

His new passion was her.

He was right. She didn't know him completely. Someone else had taken over him as he masterfully disappeared into another role. The role of master lover, one who catered to her every need, filling her with desire and also satisfying it.

But...he was a stranger. She felt as if he was hiding behind this new role. It allowed him to be intimate without being close. This intoxicating attention diverted her from his needs. He made his only focus her.

He gave her no opportunity to respond to his lust. His desires. She didn't know how to please him. Every time she tried to respond to his touch or his kiss or draw him close she felt him stiffen, pause, hesitate. He still didn't trust her, he was on guard. She couldn't penetrate his armor. Her only option was to give up and surrender.

And when Damon felt Angela's surrender he moaned in triumph. He'd won. She was his completely. To him, a woman was like a kitchen. No matter the shape or size he knew his way around it. Adored it.

It was a marvelous sacred place just as his Popa had taught him. There were few places he could be completely himself— in the kitchen and in bed with a woman. In both places he could take charge, be of service, elicit moans of ecstasy, give pleasure.

Although Angela had been a little harder to handle, the challenge had only excited him more. She didn't respond as easily as others had done. But finally she was under his spell. Her warm legs wrapped around his body, her tight center coating his erection in liquid fire.

Every hard angle of his body fit her full, soft curves.

He explored her thighs, touched her nipples with his tongue, covered her breasts with his mouth before he cupped them in his hands.

He looked up at her face eager to see a haze of passion in her eyes.

He saw her stifle a yawn.

He felt his entire body go cold.

She looked at him and bit her lip as if she'd gotten caught doing something she shouldn't have.

Which was right. She shouldn't have yawned.

Angela forced a laugh. "Did you see that?"

"Am I boring you?" Damon asked in a lethally soft voice.

"No," she said too quickly for him to believe her. "You're amazing. I'm loving this."

His jaw twitched. "You're lying."

She shifted her gaze, chewing on her lower lip. Her hesitation made his body feel even colder.

So cold he feared that if she touched him he'd shatter. This couldn't be happening. Not to him. He was an outstanding lover.

He loved women. He knew how to please them and yet Angela was telling him he was failing. Of all the women to disappoint he couldn't disappoint her.

He took a deep breath, feeling fear turning into rage. But

he couldn't be angry at her. This was his fault and he had to fix it. "Do you want to be on top?" he asked, making sure to keep his voice neural. "Do you want me to come from the back, the side? I can—"

"It's not the position."

His heart began to race. Dear God, don't let her say it was him.

"It's just that...you seem to be a breast man."

Damon paused not quite knowing how to respond. "Your breasts are beautiful. Your entire body is—"

"Thank you, the problem is my breasts aren't that sensitive so after awhile I get bored."

He began to pull away, his face burning. Never in his life had he felt so humiliated. "So I *am* boring you."

She grabbed his arm with a strength that surprised him and gave him hope. "No! It's not you. It's...what do you like?"

"What?"

She motioned to her chest. "Do you like this?"

He scowled. "Are you being sarcastic again?"

"No, I really want to know."

"Of course," he said irritated. "I wouldn't be here if—"

"Good, so tell me one thing."

He held his breath. "What?"

"How do you want me to touch you?"

He blinked. Nobody had ever asked him that before. It didn't make sense. But she was serious. There was no teasing in her gaze or her voice. Why would this matter to her? "You can touch me anyway you want. But I'm not the one who matters. I'm a guy. This comes easy to me. It's you who—"

She touched his ear with the tip of her tongue and whispered, "Do you like when I do this?"

He grimaced, trying hard not to shudder in disgust. "Not really."

"How about this?" She sucked a sensitive part behind his ear. This time his body shuddered in delight. He'd never felt that before. "Hmm, that's nice, but—"

"Shh...let's find out what else you like."

Damon began to draw away feeling uneasy. This wasn't how it was supposed to be.

But Angela didn't release her hold as she kissed along his shoulders, which didn't do much for him. But...oh damn...her nipples may not be sensitive but *his* certainly were as well as his lower abs, which he found out when he felt her slide her hot palm there.

She grinned. "You're enjoying this."

"Hmm."

She kissed him under his chin, another sensitive spot he hadn't known before. "This is what I want from you." She gently touched the side of his face. "I want to get to know you, Damon. Not the world famous chef, not the wealthy business-man, not the rich lover. You. Let me see who you are. The man I told your mother about. The man I kissed on the balcony. The man who trusts me with his secrets. Who lets me hold him when he stumbles, who's not afraid to ask for help. He's the man I want to be with."

Damon shook his head, pleasure mixing with fear. She was asking too much. "I don't know who you're talking about."

"The man I met years ago before all this." She gestured to the elegant room.

"I've always had money," he said bored.

"That's not what I mean. I'm talking about the man before the reputation he created for the world."

"He's gone."

"No, he's not. I'm starting to recognize him." She tickled under his chin.

He brushed her hand away. "Stop that."

Her eyes danced with mischief. "You like it."

"Not when I'm trying to concentrate."

"You don't have to concentrate, you just have to let go."

She was definitely asking too much. He bent down to kiss her, to stop her from speaking, but she turned her face away and his kiss landed on her cheek.

Her face remained turned from him when she finally said, "If you want me to have fun then let me do this." She looked at him, almost pleading. "I'm not lying when I say the sex has been amazing. You're a wonderful lover. But for me giving pleasure is as important as receiving it."

His pleasure. She wanted to give him pleasure. That was an entirely new territory. A place he'd never explored before.

It was a place he wanted to explore with her. He gave a faint nod and this time when he bent to kiss her she didn't turn away. Her lips met his and he succumbed to her velvet warmth.

And Angela felt no need to surrender because the man before her was no longer a stranger. The man whose body covered hers was no longer just a hot, virile and sexy lover.

He was *her* lover. A man not only attuned to her but her to him.

He was hers to claim and hers to treasure.

She'd taken a gamble and lost her heart. The man she had awakened had also awakened something dormant in her. She felt a need to feel part of someone's life who truly wanted her there.

He had the awe-inspiring magnificence, not of a demon, but of a god. He was still fiery hot but this time so was she.

They were equals, neither one afraid to singe the other in an adventurous discovery of pleasure that seemed endless.

But Jadin's soft cry reminded them both that it wasn't.

So they waited for another time to be together. And found it over and over and over again.

Until Angela's bed lay untouched for a week and she didn't miss it at all.

CHAPTER THIRTY-TWO

"**S**o when are you going shopping?"

Angela paused with her blouse halfway over her head.

She had just finished a deliciously sexy afternoon quickie with Damon who remained in bed, lounging like a king in a harem with energy to spare, but she avoided looking at him because he had a dangerous way of convincing her to stay longer than she should and she wanted to get some work done before her son woke up from his nap. "Shopping for what?"

"Clothes."

She tucked her blouse into her jeans. "You think I need new clothes?"

He nodded.

"Are you getting bored of my lingerie?"

Damon frowned. "You wear lingerie?"

Angela stared at him outraged. She lifted up her blouse to show her pink bra. "What do you think *this* is?"

He shrugged. "Underwear." He held up his hand before

she could speak. "But that's not what I mean. I'm talking about your wardrobe."

"I like my clothes," she grumbled, tucking her blouse back in. "I can't believe you insulted my bra."

"I didn't mean to." He crooked his finger. "Come here and let me make it up to you."

"Next time I'm coming in here dressed in a plaid nightdress that covers me completely."

He raised his eyebrows unconcerned. "As long as I can strip you out of it, I really don't care what you wear."

"Then why are we talking about clothes?"

"Because they're important and—"

"I don't have time to go shopping. Besides I'm focused on reviewing the present state of the DRCA. "You didn't complain when you took me to The Spicy Papaya to see how some graduates there were doing." She'd enjoyed the visit and not only for the atmosphere and the food, but because she'd gotten a chance to see Trish again and see how much the program had helped her. "I'm not ready to meet anyone else yet, but I had a good chat on the phone with Serena."

"It's not for that."

"Then why would I need a new wardrobe?"

Damon patted the space on the bed beside him as an invitation. "For the photo shoot."

Angela rested her hands on her hips, determined not to get any closer. "Why would I need a photo shoot?"

"There are also interviews. Two TV shows, three online videos and four radio shows."

"What for?"

He looked at her amused. "You're my wife, remember?"

Angela stared at him not quite understanding what he

meant. Of course she remembered she was his wife. She'd been married to him for less than three weeks and she'd already had to meet his sister, his household staff and his mother. Soon she'd have to meet the people at the DRCA and the...

Dawning slowly came to her. In all their time together she'd forgotten what he did for a living.

He was a celebrity chef. He had a business based on his personal brand.

Their marriage may have been a private affair, but Damon was still a very public personality. Not only did she have to lie to his family she had to lie to the world.

Damon noticed her hesitation and said, "If you want, I can use Vanessa as a decoy for a little while longer, but not too long."

"No need. I'll go shopping. I'm ready for this."

SHE WAS MORE THAN READY. AND THE MORNING OF THEIR first public appearance together, she showed it. Damon waited for her at the bottom of the staircase, giving Ray the final instructions on what he wanted done the rest of the week. It took him a moment to realize Ray wasn't listening to him anymore. Something above Damon's head had caught his attention. Ray wasn't a man easily distracted.

But when Damon turned around and saw Angela he did a double take. The woman slowly descending down the stairs had the bearing of a queen, the gleam of a warrior and the body of a courtesan. She wore her hair pulled back and walked to towards them as a vision of power and beauty dressed in a black and red knit pencil skirt and gold blouse.

She met him at the bottom of the stairs. "Jadin's happy with the nanny."

Damon was happy to hear that since they'd decided to keep him out of the limelight. "Are you ready?"

He had trouble getting his mouth to move. He could only manage a nod. She beamed at him. "Great. Let's go."

She was a natural. As his marketing specialist she'd been dynamo, as his wife she was ten times more fierce and savvy. She turned every opportunity into a marketing campaign without being overwhelming. She'd taken charge of the photo shoot making sure he was portrayed in the best light while also complimenting the photographer and her crew, she spoke passionately during their interviews while carefully crafting tidbits and insights that could be easily quoted and spread online.

From New York City to Boston to Toronto and DC Angela protected both him and his brand and made every public appearance a roaring success.

On a drive to one of their final scheduled appearances at a cooking competition in Rhode Island Damon closed his eyes, gathering the strength he needed. He felt tired but didn't want to show it. They'd been away from home for a week and they both missed Jadin. Plus Damon had a prescription to pick up and an upcoming doctor's appointment Vanessa had helped schedule for him with a specialist to help him deal with his loss of appetite and increased joint pain.

He felt something warm and soft cover his hand. When he opened his eyes and looked down, he saw Angela's hand covering his, the gleam of her wedding ring catching the light of the setting sun. He lifted his gaze and met her silent question with a brief, "I'm okay."

And he was. Better than okay. They made a great pair and

he was glad to have her by his side. He squeezed her hand before he kissed the back of it, wishing he could tell her how much he loved her. Wishing she loved him even a fraction as much.

But it wasn't a time for confession because he knew her biggest challenge still lay ahead.

CHAPTER THIRTY-THREE

For some revenge may be a dish best served cold, but for Angela revenge was a dish best served on a hot summer day with a French manicure, dressed in a new maroon colored tailored suit and black heels.

Damon had gathered the employees of the DRCA in the auditorium to introduce her as the new marketing specialist.

She gave a brief presentation to introduce herself and give them an idea of some of the changes that would happen over the next several months to put the program on more solid footing. She welcomed their feedback and gave her contact information before she ended her speech to open the floor for questions.

"It's a pleasure to meet you," Ricardo said coming up to her at the end of the session. He looked less formidable outside of the classroom, his pitch black dyed hair and wiry frame more comical than fierce. He greeted her with an enthusiasm that made it clear he didn't recognize her.

But she recognized him.

Less than a year ago she'd left this building in tears after he'd humiliated her in his classroom, he'd seen her as a shabbily dressed pregnant woman with little prospects.

Now she'd returned slimmer, fashionably dressed and the wife of the owner and better than that—she had power.

She smiled down at him, her heels giving her a few inches of height. "We've met before."

He shook his head. "I don't think so. I'd remember someone like you."

"Someone whose best is the worst you've ever seen? Someone who doesn't belong here?"

The dawning of realization on Ricardo's face was sweet revenge. He looked horrified at first then terrified.

His life was in her hands.

With one word to Human Resources or Damon for that matter, his job could be on the chopping block.

He blinked quickly, rubbing his hands together. "It was never my intention to—"

He stopped when Damon came up behind her. "Sorry to interrupt, but there are a few things I want to show you before we go."

"I'll be right there," she said. "I'm just catching up with an old acquaintance."

"You know each other?"

"Yes," Angela said.

Ricardo flashed a sickly grin. "A little."

"He taught me a lot."

Damon nodded pleased and patted him on the back. "I'm glad to hear that. Ricardo was one of our first hires. It took a lot of convincing to get him to join us. I'm glad he did."

"I have a few things to say to him, then I'll be right there."

Angela waited for Damon to be out of hearing before her expression changed from professionally cordial to menacing.

"If you're going to fire me, make it quick." He folded his arms, trying to look nonchalant. Instead he looked scared. Being fired in such a soft market would be difficult, but losing Damon's respect and perhaps his reputation in the industry would be much worse.

Angela shook her head. "I'm not going to fire you, but I will issue you a warning. People come to this program for a chance at a better life not for someone to look down on them and make them feel inferior. Before you humiliated me I worked on huge marketing campaigns with budgets that would make your eyes water. I was a professional with a life I'd worked hard to build.

"Some poor choices and life circumstances brought me to your classroom. I was desperate."

"I didn't mean—"

"I wasn't lying when I told Damon I learned a lot from you. At this moment I realized that the high flying professional, the nearly broke mother-to-be, and the woman who is standing in front of you right now are the same. Her circumstances may have changed, but her worth never did."

She leaned in closer and lowered her voice. "From now on be very careful how you treat people, sometimes your actions may come around to bite you." She snapped her teeth together in emphasis—her white teeth even more prominent against her dark purple lipstick. "Your circumstances can change too. If I hear you mistreat someone I'll bite down hard and give you the same mercy you gave me. Are we clear?"

Ricardo nodded looking properly chagrined.

Angela turned on her heel and left.

"Should I be jealous?" Damon asked her when she joined him near the exit.

"Of who?"

"Ricardo. You looked like you wanted to devour him."

She looped her arm through his, preening in victory. "Oh, that was nothing. Just gave him a few things to chew on."

CHAPTER THIRTY-FOUR

Orange streaks of autumn sunlight slid through the blinds of the nursery dousing the room in a hazy warm glow as Damon finished Jadin's bath one evening. He sat on the ground next to the green tub. A towel, diaper, baby lotion on hand for when he was through.

With a giggle of delight, Jadin lifted one tiny hand and slashed the water sending soap into Damon's face.

"Help, I think he blinded me."

Angela uncurled her legs and left the chair where she'd been sitting and typing on her laptop. "Don't be dramatic," she scolded him, then took a cotton ball and dabbed the soap from his eyes. "It's tear-free soap."

"Never can be too careful."

She returned to her seat and picked up her laptop. "He'll soon be big enough for the main bath."

"Yeah," Damon said but preferred holding that off a little while longer. Being with Jadin like this was one of his truest pleasures. Jadin was such a calm, happy baby. Rubbing his chubby little body in the warm water, the scent of coconut oil and the sound of gently splashing water had almost become like a meditation to him. Although they traded off days bathing him, Angela was always nearby reading or working.

She and Jadin both gave him a feeling of home.

Damon gently picked the baby up and carefully placed him down on the towel. A wet baby could be a very slippery thing and the last thing he wanted to do was drop him. Damon always inwardly sighed in relief when he safely wrapped Jadin up in a towel.

He thoroughly dried him off then put him in a diaper and clothes for the night. "Success."

"You don't have to announce that each time."

"I know you're here with me to supervise."

Angela sent him a knowing look. "That's not why I'm here."

"It's not?"

"No. I like watching you bathe him." She wiggled her eyebrows. "Especially since you like to do it with your shirt off."

He looked down at his bare chest. "I don't like getting my shirt wet."

"What is it with you and getting your clothes soiled?"

He shrugged. "I'm part cat."

"There are ways around getting wet."

"I'll stick to my method."

"That's fine." She winked. "I like your method."

Damon chuckled before he put his shirt back on and buttoned it up. She might enjoy watching him, but he enjoyed watching her more. Especially with Jadin. She was a wonderful mother—attentive, nurturing, caring. She'd hum silly songs to him while she bathed him, and loved carrying him in her arms around the garden and point flowers and plants out to him, and she'd applaud his small triumphs like sitting up on his own, and soothe him when he cried.

She was all the things his own mother had never been to him.

His wife was a caring woman.

His wife. It surprised him how much he liked admitting that fact.

Although his family was still adjusting to his marriage, he'd gotten used to it. His mother was no longer an issue and his father had never shown any concern, Helen didn't really count, but Leo surprised him. Despite Angela's success keeping Damon's profile solid, his brand marketable, his brother Leo had continued to be wary of her.

"Why are you letting her be in charge?" he'd asked Damon one day after Angela had launched a crowdfunding campaign for the DRCA program. He and Leo had concluded a successful business meeting, following years of negotiations, with a company that wanted to license his brand on their line of dinnerware. They now sat together in Leo's office, which smelled like tennis balls freshly popped from the can and strawberry-lemon flavored gummies.

Damon took pride in keeping his life—and the people in it —compartmentalized. He had an almost religious devotion to the French culinary phrase *mise in place*: meaning everything in its place.

Ray took care of his home affairs.

Angela focused on his non-profit while Leo focused on the rest. With effort, he'd managed to keep them apart and Angela —thankfully—had been too busy to notice. Unfortunately, he wasn't so lucky with his brother who kept tabs of everything she did. "I thought the DRCA program was your baby."

Damon leaned back in his chair, until the front legs were

off the ground. He knew that always annoyed his brother. "What's the problem? I thought you wanted me to focus on other projects."

Leo clasped his hands together on his desk. "I just didn't think you'd let her take the lead like you did in the past."

Damon rocked back and forth on the back legs, hiding a grin when his brother furrowed his brows. "I trust her. If she can't salvage the program, if it doesn't work she'll shut it down, but I think it needs fresh new eyes."

"Stop doing that."

Damon leaned a little farther feigning innocence. "What?"

"You'd never do that if Mom were here."

He started to rock again. "No, but she's not."

Leo glared at him. "Cut it out."

Damon set the chair on all four legs. "Better?"

Leo folded his arms but looked relieved. "I'm not sure. You've really been acting strange recently. A new wife, a new kid and then letting her take over your life—"

"She's not taking over anything, she's sharing it. I wanted someone to share my life with, that's why I married her."

His brother stared at him. "Are you sure there isn't something else going on?" He let his arms fall. "You'd tell me, wouldn't you?"

Damon sighed. He didn't like lying to his brother but he had to. Before it was to protect himself, now he had more at stake. Angela and Jadin meant too much to him to let anyone interfere. "I just thought it was time."

"Well, you've put me in a bad position. Now both Joyce and Mom are pressuring me for a wedding date. And she's talking babies." He shuddered.

Damon thought of his brother's longtime girlfriend with pity. "Do you want to marry her?"

"Eventually."

Damon studied his brother for a moment then said in a quiet voice, "Does eventually include this century?"

"Maybe another couple years."

He sighed recognizing the truth. "You're being unfair to her. Let her down gently."

Leo shook his head looking miserable. "It's not that I don't want to get married. I just don't want to get married yet."

"And maybe she's not the one."

He sniffed. "I don't believe in that. I think you find someone compatible and make it work."

"If that's the case then what difference will a couple years make? Marry her now." When a look of panic crossed his brother's face he added, "What are you afraid of? Is there someone else?"

"I don't have the time."

"Then what?"

He shrugged, sounding lost. "I don't know."

"You'd better tell her."

"I don't want to hurt her and I do love her."

Damon hesitated then said, "Mom met Angela and then said I did well." He nodded when Leo stared at him in disbelief. "Really. Angela got her to say it."

"Mom said it with her mouth?"

Damon sent his brother a scorching look. "How else would she say it?"

"Maybe it was a ventriloquist trick. Angela's crafty."

"It wasn't."

Leo took a deep breath. "So you're saying I should get married to make Mom happy?"

Damon shook his head. "No, I'm saying, I followed my

instincts and it worked out. If marrying Joyce is what you truly want to do it won't be a burden."

Damon thought of what he'd told his brother as he looked at Angela. Being with this woman wasn't a struggle. It felt natural. Marrying her had been one of the smartest decisions he'd made.

Angela suddenly snapped her fingers and pointed at him.

"You could be one way to generate extra income."

"Why would I need extra income?" It had been nearly four months since she'd made her presentation at the DRCA program and through a savvy crowdfunding campaign on a newly launched platform, a well publicized cooking face off with two categories featuring both amateurs and professionals, his nonprofit had not only become solvent but had enough funds to run for at least two more years.

"For the program of course."

"You've already succeeded—"

"The greatest threat to future success is current success. I don't want to leave any options for failure open. And you're the ticket."

"Me?"

"Yes, ever thought of charging for someone to spend one day with you?"

His brows shot up and he crossed his arms over his chest like a shy virgin. "I'm a married man."

She frowned at him. "Not like that. As a chef. There are people who would pay for you to give them tips. One-on-one. Let's say we'd limit it to five sessions. Two people at a time. We could charge a deliciously exorbitant amount and that money could go to the program."

He began to shake his head.

"That is just one idea. We could also think of publishing a

specialty cook book, including select recipes from some of the courses. You change the courses up every year so the special edition could be an annual thing." She snapped her fingers. "Better yet, people could bid to have a dish named after them. That would be fun."

Damon picked up the soft rattle with a smiling elephant head and waved it in Jadin's face, letting the baby grab it when he reached for it. "People wouldn't pay for that."

"You'd be surprised what people will pay for. There's always a certain type of consumer who will pay to be made to feel special. If we market it right, it can be very lucrative. They could choose an appetizer, main meal or dessert. Or perhaps they don't get a choice. Maybe we'll make it just a dessert."

He folded his arms. "Not really my specialty."

"It's just an idea," Angela said jotting down some notes. "I have to think of the future. Next year you could..." Her words fell away and she looked at him with a mixture of sadness and horror as she remembered he didn't have another year.

He didn't want her to look at him like that. He didn't want to make her sad. "It's okay. I like your optimism."

"I'm sorry."

"Don't be." He picked Jadin up and placed him in his crib before he went to the baby tub dipped his hand in then play-fully sprinkled her with his wet hand. "I like that you want to keep me around."

She wiped the water from her face. "Damon—"

He picked up the tub. "I've got to clean this." He walked into the bathroom and emptied it out. He thoroughly cleaned it, telling himself he was scrubbing it extra hard because it was important not because he was angry, then returned back to the nursery. He stopped when he noticed that Angela had cleared the rest of the items on the ground so that he didn't have to.

She motioned that the baby was asleep and that they should both leave the room.

He waited for her in the hall. Once she'd gently closed the door he said, "What dessert would you like named after you?"

She shrugged avoiding his gaze and headed down the hall. "I don't know. Doesn't matter. We're not talking about me."

"I'd name a chocolate mousse after you."

She stared at him stunned. "You think I look like a moose?"

The tension inside him ebbed, if she was teasing him she was okay. He rubbed his chin in thought. "Angela's decadent double fudge brownie."

"Hmm." She walked down the stairs. "Not bad."

"With lava chocolate center with just the faintest hint of raspberry sauce." He winked at her. "Something like that."

She shot him a look over her shoulder. "With a little less innuendo." She headed for the kitchen.

"Innuendos are fun." He tapped his chest. "Okay, my turn. What dessert would you name after me?"

Angela placed her laptop on the kitchen table and sat. "I'm not a baker. I don't know."

Damon took the seat in front of her. "Neither am I. Come on. You can guess. You eat enough to know." He held up his hands. "And that's not an insult so don't look at me like that."

She sighed. "Okay, a dessert...Damon's cherry pie."

He made a face. "Cherry pie?"

"Yes."

"Sweet but unassuming with a warm filling."

"That's not exactly sexy."

"No, but I'd savor every bite."

He shook his head. "I don't like cherry pie, think of something else."

"No."

"Please."

She rolled her eyes. "Okay, how about Damon's tapioca pudding."

"Are you trying to hurt my feelings?"

"I love tapioca. What is wrong with you?"

"I name a dessert after you that people will be thinking about for days and you give me two bland ideas."

"They're not bland. Tapioca is delicious and cherry pie... hmm. You just haven't experienced the right ones. I'll buy you one and—"

"Frozen? No thanks."

"Don't be a snob."

"I'm not a fan of frozen pies."

"Well, as you know, I don't cook so you'll have to deal with it."

Damon playfully groaned, knowing he'd never tell her that he'd deal with a lot to keep her from thinking about him dying.

CHAPTER THIRTY-FIVE

*W*hoosh!!

Leo swung his racket and hit the tennis ball with as much force as possible. He imagined each ball from the indoor tennis court machine had Angela's face on it. The exercise was therapeutic.

A trip to his sports club usually was, but this time he needed it more than ever.

Whoosh!!

Angela Watkins was never supposed to get close to his brother again.

Now she was his wife.

But Leo knew who she truly was. His brother was blind. That woman was ruining his life again. Damon wasn't acting like himself. He wasn't working the way he'd used to. He focused more on managerial aspects of the business when before he only cared about being with people—mentoring young chefs, public appearances, being in the kitchen. His brother's once energetic pace had dramatically slowed. Instead of a busy traveling scheduled, he preferred staying close to home.

With his wife and son.

Whoosh!!

Unfortunately, Angela wasn't only ruining Damon's life, but his own. His brother's marriage had really spurred Joyce. Now marriage was all Joyce kept talking about.

Leo sighed. His brother was right. He didn't know what was stopping him. He didn't want to do the responsible thing. He wanted to be free. He didn't envision a life with a wife and kids and the house and trust funds. That was all right for many, but he wasn't sure it was right for him. Even though he acted like it was. He knew that was why Joyce had chosen him. "You're so dependable," she'd said, like it was a compliment.

Whoosh!!

But he didn't want to be. Sometimes he wanted to just jump on a plane and see where it took him.

Sometimes he wanted to be someone else.

His brother had the boldness to breakaway. Leo hadn't ever thought of it. As the eldest, he'd gotten his parents' full attention. He was to fulfill his parents' every desire and he had, not realizing that the price he'd pay was to be invisible. He was supposed to take over the family business but his parents nudged him to 'look after' Damon, which was how he'd become his manager.

He was his father's son, Damon's brother and manager, Joyce' fiancé. Nobody knew him. Nobody really cared to know him and the worst of it was he didn't exactly know himself.

What he did know was that his brother was up to something. That his brother was changing his life and it was encouraging Leo to do the same. To not worry if it didn't work out. Just to try.

Whoosh!!

He had to face his fears.

LEO HADN'T CHANGED.

Angela didn't know why that was the first thing that came to her mind when he entered the office she'd set up at the DRCA program. He was a good looking man she'd always thought she would like, if he didn't hate her. Why he'd taken a dislike to her she never knew, but didn't care since Damon had been her client and not him. But he was an easy man to ignore, he faded to the background whenever Damon was in the room.

She'd been surprised when he'd made an appointment to see her. She'd been so busy the past several months she'd forgotten about him and the lies he'd told Damon about her. She was glad to get a chance to confront him.

"Thanks for seeing me," he said with a nod. A true gentleman raised by parents who expected it. He was always very polite, a trait Angela always used to her advantage.

"Why did you lie about me?" she said, taking him off guard.

She saw a flash of surprise then anger in his eyes before he said in a tone as smooth as silk, "I don't know what you're talking about."

"You told Damon I said he was pathetic. That the ideas he had I gave to him."

"You did say that."

"No, I didn't."

"Yes, you did." He sniffed amused. "It's too late to hide the truth. Your boyfriend told me everything."

"My boyfriend?"

"Yes, the guy you were seeing at the time."

"Ronald? You spoke to Ronald?"

Leo nodded. "He was very forthright about everything that happened. I tried to reach you on your cell phone because my brother had thought he'd made a mistake leaving your firm and that guy answered your phone and told me there was no point in trying to change things. He told me how you really felt."

She couldn't believe it. Ronald had lied about her? She'd never believed Megan's suspicion that Ronald had been jealous of Damon until now. He'd ruined her chances of getting Damon back as a client.

She pounded her desk, causing Leo to jump in surprise. "You idiot!"

"What?"

"Why didn't you confront me?"

"Why would I do that?"

"Because...oh I don't know, this is just a crazy guess... maybe—" She stopped. She planned to give him a sarcastic reply then remembered the Branson family didn't take sarcasm well and it was a time to be honest. "Ronald was lying to you."

Leo frowned perplexed. "Why would he lie?"

"Because." Angela stopped and sighed not sure how to explain what she was still grappling with. The man she'd loved and had once planned to marry had tried to destroy her career. It had only been recently that she'd seen how toxic their relationship had been. There had been small things she hadn't wanted to see because she hadn't wanted to lose him.

But now that he was gone, she realized his little jokes about her looks and ambitions were more hurtful than humorous. She now knew how much he'd made sure she was dependant on him. She'd never questioned their long engagement, his name on the house deed, his choice of where they vacationed, where they dined. What she'd once thought of as compromise had truly been surrender. Surrendering to him. But as a proud career woman she'd never seen it that way. However, one area Ronald couldn't touch was her career. She'd never let him dissuade her from working with Damon, she'd never imagined what a threat he'd seen in him. "Ronald was angry at me," Angela said, knowing it was an overly simplistic explanation. "This was a way to get back at me."

Leo looked at her for a long moment then called Ronald a series of foul words that would have had his mother swooning and had Angela staring at him in shock.

"He made a fool of me," he said.

"No, he tricked you and me too. The point is Ronald was wrong. I never once thought or said those things about Damon. Ever. I loved working with your brother. Even you when you weren't being a complete stick in the mud."

He hesitated. "Really?"

"Yes."

"I'm sorry. I was wrong. I just wasn't sure you were always good for Damon."

"Why not?"

He paused. "Why did you marry him?"

"You didn't answer my question."

"I will once you answer mine."

"What does the reason why I married him have to do with anything?"

"It goes to my point. You were—are—able to convince my brother to do outrageous things."

"Not really, he—"

"Not long ago my brother was a committed bachelor. He meets you again after years and then...Boom! He becomes a doting husband and father."

Angela shifted in her chair, uncomfortable. "It was more his idea than mine. We didn't realize how much we cared—uh-loved each other until now," she said but Leo wasn't listening.

Instead he was staring down at his lap, tapping his thumbs together. "That was what always made me nervous about you. From the first moment you were like no one we'd ever met before. My family thought Damon's ideas were ridiculous." He stared at her. "But you never did. That's why you sometimes made me nervous. You have this strange way of making the impossible seem possible. I never thought there'd be a way to save DRCA. I never imagined a guy who liked to cook could create a mini empire out of it. I thought he was crazy. But he's happier than I am." Leo tapped his chest. "Which isn't fair because I have done everything right. I did everything that's been expected of me and soon I'm going to have to get married."

"You don't have to stay unhappy."

He gazed up at the ceiling, a sour grin on his face. "There you go trying to convince me of the impossible."

"It's not impossible to change your life. It just takes effort. And courage."

He met her gaze. "That's what I don't have."

"Do you really not want to get married?"

"I don't know anymore." He sighed. "Since you've reentered Damon's life it's like he's a new person. I wonder if that's what I'm missing. If—"

"No, he's not happier because of me. The happiness was already there. He loves what he does. He loves what he's built. I added to his life, but I don't make up his life. You have to figure out what you want. No one can give that to you. Expecting that from anyone is unfair. Marriage isn't just about meeting the right person, it's about *being* the right person. Don't force yourself into a box that doesn't suit you."

Leo gripped his hand into a fist. "You're right. I'm being unfair. Damon said the same. It's time for me to come clean." He stood and held out his hand. "I'm glad we had this discussion."

Angela couldn't suppress a grin as she looked at his outstretched hand. "There's no need to be so formal. We're family now."

"Yes, right, but...um...I don't hug."

"Very well." She shook his hand. "It was great seeing you again."

He nodded then took a step back. "Since we are family now, if there was anything wrong with Damon you'd let me know, right?"

Angela swallowed. His gaze was probing. She'd underestimated him. He may disappear in Damon's shadow, but he was a keen observer. "Why should anything be wrong?"

His gaze remained steady. "It's just a question. I'm hoping nothing is wrong."

"Me too because I'm happy. I'd hate for anything to ruin that."

"I see." He turned and Angela breathed a sigh of relief. The Branson men had a look that could bore through steel. Damon certainly knew his brother when he stood up for him and said he didn't lie. It was heartening to know he was someone she could trust—unlike her ex.

But she didn't want to waste her time thinking about Ronald right now. Her life may have been derailed but now she was back on track. She had a job she enjoyed, she could provide for her son and she was in a relationship with a man who not only encouraged her ambitions but supported them. It still amazed her how seamlessly their lives had become intertwined. How she never felt alone.

She remembered one harried, exhausting afternoon when she'd been working from home, because it was the nanny's day off and Jadin had been in a fussy mood, crying on and off since the morning.

After feeding him lunch he had another crying fit and she felt her patience thinning because she had a conference call with Serena and the notes she had on the kitchen table had to be organized plus she'd managed to eat only a handful of nuts since morning because she hadn't taken the time to eat breakfast. So she'd picked him up and tried to calm him by pacing the kitchen, but his crying only seemed to grow louder.

She felt Damon's presence behind her before he softly said the sweetest words, "Give him to me. Don't worry. I've got this."

Angela handed Jadin to him feeling a twinge of guilt. "I just need an hour—"

"Take your time," Damon said before he left the kitchen, giving her the space and peace she needed.

A couple hours later, when she'd finished the main tasks for the day, she went and found Damon in the family room taking Jadin out of his swing. "Look," he said, "Mommy's here."

"Thanks. I'm glad you were home today." He usually wasn't. Once they'd announced their marriage his schedule of obligations seemed to have increased.

He shrugged. "It was nice."

She looked at Jadin surprised he was wearing different clothes. "He really likes you. I couldn't get him to calm down."

"It wasn't me. It was…"

"What?" she pressed when his words faded away.

"The shirt was too tight. He'd outgrown it and the sleeves were biting into his arms."

Tears sprung to her eyes. She hadn't noticed that. Her son hadn't been miserable for no reason, he had been in pain and she hadn't noticed. What kind of mother—

"No," Damon said in a firm voice as if reading her mind. "Don't do that to yourself. It was an accident. And look at him. He's okay."

Jadin may be okay, but she felt awful. Tears fell.

"Mommy's sad. Give her a hug," Damon said to Jadin. Her son stretched his arms out to her.

Angela held him close, trying her best not to drown him in her tears. She inhaled the sweet scent of his baby shampoo. "I'm so sorry. Mommy's so sorry."

"He forgives you." Damon placed a kiss on her cheek then whispered, "Now stop crying or he's going to start to worry and not understand why."

She sniffed and took a deep breath. She stared at Jadin and cupped his chubby cheek. He was almost a year now, but her beautiful little boy stared at her uncertain. Damon was right, she didn't want to confuse him.

She made a funny face and he giggled. She shifted her gaze to Damon, her heart filled with gratitude and love. "I don't know what I'll do without you," she said then regretted her words because an expression of sadness and longing briefly crossed his face. "You'll manage."

Angela sat back in her office chair and remembered that she'd held him tight that night and he'd let her. She'd inhaled his scent, pressed her cheek against his warm skin, skimmed her hand along the slope of his shoulders, tickled her nose against the tight curls at the nape of his neck, and listened to the sound of his breathing.

It had been weeks since that moment and she'd let it fade to memory, but Leo's visit had brought it back to her. He'd made her remember that she and Damon did have something special; something that wouldn't last.

However as she now sat alone in her office she realized something else. Something that made a shadow of icy darkness creep into her heart.

She realized that she'd been so busy she hadn't noticed she hadn't heard or seen Damon for the past three days.

CHAPTER THIRTY-SIX

He deserved the slap. But Leo didn't think he deserved the broken vase.

"Five years!" Joyce screeched. "I've given you five years of my life and you don't want to marry me?"

He'd probably handled it wrong, starting with the location. Perhaps he should have chosen a more public place instead of his apartment.

Leo sat ramrod straight on his couch and inwardly sighed at the sight of the shattered glass—offering a glass of white wine also probably hadn't been wise, but he'd thought it would relax her—and broken vase on the hardwood floor. Yes, the location had been a mistake and costly. He tapped his thumbs together as another thought struck him.

He probably shouldn't have told her that he'd changed his mind and that she deserved someone else. His word choice had been all wrong, but he could rectify that. He had to.

"I do want to marry you," he said quickly, even though it was a lie, "just not yet and I don't think it's fair—"

The sound of shattering ceramic cut through his words, he

stared at the broken remnants of the plate she'd thrown on the ground. The vegetable platter had likely also been a poor choice. But she was dieting again and he'd forgotten whether she'd cut out sweets or fats this time.

"Fair?" Her voice cracked. "You want to talk about fair when I had to put up with you with the slim hope you'd grow a spine?"

"Hey, now wait—"

"Listening to you drone on about your mother, your boring discussions about your brother. The handsome one. The talented one. But I was willing to swallow it all. And look what it got me. Nothing."

Leo stood. He had to take control of this situation. Angela told him he needed courage. "Joyce, I—"

She took a menacing step towards him, icy contempt etched in her face. He sank back into his seat. Courage would have to wait. "No, you're not breaking up with me. You'll never breakup with me. I've invested too much into this relationship. I don't care what I have to do. I'm almost thirty-five. Time isn't on my side. If I have to get your mother to hound you every day I will."

Leo shivered. "You wouldn't."

"I would. She likes me. She's looking forward to having me as a daughter-in-law and I don't plan to disappoint her. My parents are also waiting. They are so happy for me. So you can get over this little crisis of yours." He winced when she smiled and patted his cheek. Her voice softened. "I forgive you. Your brother got married and you're getting married too. Get used to it."

She walked over and picked up her purse that she'd placed on the side table. She pulled out her wallet. "Your housekeeper comes today, right?"

He nodded.

She handed him a twenty dollar bill. "Give this to her." When Leo stared at her blankly, Joyce glanced at the broken items and added, "To compensate for our little misunderstanding."

"Hmm."

Joyce set her purse down before she rested her hands on his thighs and peered into his face. "I'm never letting you go," she said in a quiet voice that was more threat than promise. She pressed her lips against his, which had all the tenderness of a hornet's sting, then sauntered out.

Leo sank back against the couch cushions and swore. Just as he thought, listening to Angela had gotten him into trouble.

CHAPTER THIRTY-SEVEN

Angela told herself nothing was wrong as she drove home that evening.

But her thoughts so distracted her that she missed her turn for a direct route home and ended up taking a longer route through the neighborhood she'd grown used to while living in Serena's basement. She passed by the convenience store and saw that the parking lot was fuller than it had been. It seemed Mr. Kim had implemented some of her ideas.

Angela slowed a little when a police cruiser passed her and almost missed the woman sitting in the back seat.

A woman she recognized by her stringy brown hair.

Becky!

She hung her head defeated.

She'd taken one risk too many.

Angela shook her head in regret as she turned down another street. Their lives had taken different paths.

But she couldn't afford to think about the past. Where was Damon now?

Damon still hadn't responded to her text detailing her talk with Leo. That worried her.

No matter how busy their schedules had been they managed to communicate, at least within a day with an email, text, note, message...something.

When she'd checked his schedule she'd noticed he'd returned from a meeting in Manila several days ago so he was supposed to be around.

But she hadn't heard anything from him. When she spoke to his grim faced personal assistant, he didn't have anything to add either since he hadn't been working with Damon for the past month.

She didn't know about that change either.

She didn't want to overreact so Angela decided against calling his mother and she didn't want to concern Leo in case nothing was really wrong.

The only person she could think of contacting was Vanessa.

After a couple rings a familiar voice said, "What's wrong, Angela?"

She hesitated. "Why would anything be wrong?"

"Because you've never called me before."

It was no use pretending. If something was wrong she needed to find out what it was. "When's the last time you heard from Damon?"

"About a week. Why?"

"It's just strange that he's been in town and I haven't heard anything."

She heard Vanessa sigh. "I don't know if I should tell you this."

"What?"

"Have you talked to Ray?"

"No, why would I talk to Ray?"

"I think you should."

"What aren't you telling me?"

"Talk to Ray first then I'll fill in the blanks if you need me to. If you really want to know, you may have to ask Ray. There are some things Damon won't even tell me."

ANGELA EXPECTED TO HAVE TO BRIBE OR THREATEN RAY to get him to tell her where Damon was, but instead he looked at her for a heartstoppingly long moment before he simply said, "He has a secret room."

A series of questions popped into her mind. Why would he need a secret room? How often has he used it? The times she'd thought he was away, was he really here in this large house without her knowing? She threw these questions at Ray but he refused to reply.

Instead he led her towards the back of the house, up a set of narrow stairs to a door that led to the attic. He nodded towards the door before he turned.

"Where are you going?" she asked when he headed down the stairs.

"You don't need me," Ray said over his shoulder, "and he probably won't forgive me for this." Ray stopped at the bottom of the stairs but he didn't look at her. "Good luck," he said before he disappeared down the hall.

Angela turned back to the door, anxiety gnawing at her. She grabbed the door handle then paused. This was Damon's private room, there was a reason he hadn't told her about it. He had his secrets and she needed to respect that. She had only wanted to know where he was. She knew that now, she didn't need to go any further.

She let her hand fall and turned.

But knowing where he was didn't mean he was all right. And why had Ray been so willing to tell her? Was something wrong?

Angela took a deep breath and opened the door. She'd face his anger.

But he wasn't there.

The large oak bed sat empty, crumpled bed sheets scattered across it.

However, not his absence nor the unmade bed shocked her as much as how small the room was. Every other room in the house was grand and large, but this one was strangely quaint. There wasn't much inside. A tiny window let in a faded stream of light, a long dresser covered with a series of medicine bottles caught her attention more than the large oak bed that almost swallowed up any remaining space in the room.

Tears choked her throat as her gaze skimmed over the various bottles. He'd been hiding so much from her and she'd let him. She'd allowed herself to forget that he was sick. Very sick.

She picked up a few bottles curious to discover what they were for, but quickly set them down when she heard the rush of running water. She turned to a door she hadn't noticed before. The room was so small she'd never imagined a bathroom would be attached to it. But it made sense if he didn't want to be seen.

And right now she didn't want him to see her. She inched towards the exit then paused when she heard the water abruptly stop.

She could hear her own breathing in the resulting silence.

She froze when the bathroom door opened.

It opened outward, hiding her, but she saw him clearly as he limped his way over to the bed. He only wore boxers and for a moment she almost covered her eyes. Not because he was almost naked—she'd seen him fully naked before—but because of how vulnerable he looked. Every painful step made her heart ache. His usually erect body was stooped like a wounded animal.

She saw him grimace, and he grabbed the bed frame, hanging his head and swearing.

She didn't feel right spying on him like this. He didn't know she was there and she didn't want him to know. He was a proud man and this would devastate him. She'd wait until he was asleep and then creep out of the room.

At least that had been her plan, but she'd forgotten she'd left her cell phone on.

It sprang to life with a call from Megan. Angela quickly turned it off.

Too late.

Her cover was blown.

Damon turned towards her, but the swift motion was too much for him and he grabbed his side and fell to his knees in pain.

Angela rushed over to him. "Are you okay?"

"What are you doing here?" he said through clenched teeth.

She touched his bare back, feeling his body tremble. Whether from pain or anger she wasn't sure and didn't care, she wasn't leaving him now. "I was worried about you."

"You're not supposed to be here."

"I threatened Ray." She held out her hand. "Let me help you up."

Damon pushed her hand away, and shot her a fierce look. "No." He carefully rose to his feet with the aid of the bed frame. "I'm okay. I have bad days sometimes."

"Why are you hurting? What's going on? How can I help?"

"I don't need help." He glanced at the row of bottles on the dresser, his face grim. "I see you've been admiring my collection."

"What is going on?"

"I get spasms sometimes, which is a side effect of another medicine I'm taking." He smiled without humor. "Fortunately, I have medication for that, so the pain will end soon. But one of the side effects of the pain medication is drowsiness so I'll be asleep in a few minutes."

"Why didn't you tell me you were—"

He crawled into bed. "I promised you wouldn't see me like this."

"I don't mind."

He rested back. "I do. You can go now."

She pulled the sheet and blanket up to his chin. "Not yet."

Damon closed his eyes and shook his head, his voice resigned. "I'm too tired to fight you."

"Good." Angela placed a tender kiss on his forehead. "Rest instead."

He opened his eyes, even clouded with sleepiness there was an intensity in his gaze. "This isn't over."

She grinned. "Yes, it is."

"Please go."

"Go to sleep and I will."

"Promise?"

"No," she whispered, but she had no fear of him hearing her because he'd fallen asleep.

CHAPTER THIRTY-EIGHT

*D*amon opened his eyes and looked around the room, a stab of pain piercing him. Of course she was gone. He'd told her to go, even though he hadn't meant it. Even though he'd been so happy to see her (something so surprising and deep it nearly burst through his anger and fear that she'd caught him at his lowest) that he'd almost forgotten the physical pain that gripped him.

Almost.

The pain had won.

The drugs had won.

He couldn't fight them and had fallen asleep. Now Angela was gone.

He glanced at the ceiling, surprised it wasn't covered in darkness. The lights were on. Hmm...he didn't remember turning the lights on, but he must have at some point before going back to sleep. The medicine always made his memory hazy.

But it hadn't blocked her out. He still remembered the shock of finding her in his room and telling her to go when he'd wanted nothing more than to ask her to stay. But she couldn't and he was glad she'd finally left. His heart was a tangled mess of contradictions.

What had he expected? Had he really expected her to stay with him all night? Had he really been so foolish to think she'd sit by his bedside and touch his forehead and worry about him the way his mother never had? She had Jadin to look after and work to do. She had a lot more important things in her life than him.

Damon sat up then froze when he saw Angela asleep with her head resting on her folded arms. She slept on the corner of his bed. She was there?

She was there!

He reached out to touch her then pulled his hand away, his heart pounding. Joy shouldn't feel this dangerous. Making his heart feel as if it would burst. She turned her head and he quickly fell back down and closed his eyes. He heard her yawn, felt the bed lighten as she lifted her head, and heard her clothes shift as she lifted her arms above her head. He swallowed. She would leave now as if nothing had happened. But as much as he didn't want her to go yet, he wouldn't open his eyes, he didn't want to embarrass her. He'd pretend to sleep.

He didn't hear her footsteps and nearly jumped when he sensed her standing beside the bed. He steeled himself when he felt her warm fingers against his forehead. Sweet torture. She touched the back of her palm to his neck then gently pulled up the blankets. He couldn't take it anymore. He opened his eyes.

She looked at him startled and stepped back. "Oh, you're awake."

He grabbed her wrist. "I told you to leave."

She patted his hand. "You're still too weak to fight me."

He tightened his hold. "I don't want to fight. I want..." He paused, swallowed, released her. "I want..." He sighed, finding and saying the words was harder than he thought. Perhaps it was better left unsaid. "Where's Jadin?"

"Asleep, but he came to visit. He even crawled all over you and played with your nose but you didn't seem to mind."

He shook his head, wondering at her sense of humor when he noticed something near his shoulder. It was Jadin's soft rattle, the elephant face smiling at him. He *had* been there!

Damon turned to Angela alarmed. "You brought him here to see me?"

"Of course. I wanted him to see his dad."

His dad. Damon felt his heart expand and constrict at the same time. He missed him.

"Go on," Angela said softly. "Tell me what you want."

He swallowed again.

"Are you thirsty? Do you want something to drink?"

"No, it's not... Would you do me a favor? It will only take a minute."

"What is it?"

He motioned her closer. "Don't laugh."

"I can't promise that, but I'll try."

He patted the space near him. "Could you sit here with me for a minute?"

Angela grinned and did. "Oh, like your mom used to do?"

Damon shook his head. "My mom never did that."

She rolled her eyes. "Okay, your dad then."

"No."

She frowned. "Then who looked after you when you got sick?"

"I didn't get sick."

"Of course you got sick. No kid can escape childhood without a fever, a cold or something."

"You can when you're not allowed."

"That doesn't make any sense. Tell me honestly. What did you do when you got sick?"

Damon took a deep breath. It was hard to share, but he wanted her to understand him. "The first time I got sick I didn't know any better so I got in trouble. I got told off and then put under a hot shower to get the toxins out. I was told that I was a germ attractor and that I hadn't cleaned my hands enough. I soon learned to lie. It's easy to deny what you don't want to acknowledge. I once had a fever so high I sweat through my clothes at dinner, my parents didn't say a word. I learned quickly how to respond. A cold was an indication of a weak constitution, a headache a luxury. They saw illness as a way to gain sympathy and they weren't having that.

So no, I didn't get sick. But I'd always wanted, just once, to have what I saw on TV—when the kid was sick in bed and the parent would sit on the side and read to them. So it'd be nice if..." Damon briefly closed his eyes embarrassed. "I know it's stupid..."

"Shh...it's not stupid. Keep your eyes closed," she said when he looked at her.

"No," he said in a deep tone. "I want to remember this."

"Okay, could you excuse me for a minute?" She stood. "I'll be right back."

Daniel watched Angela hurry into the bathroom, realizing he'd done the one thing he'd feared.

He'd driven her away.

CHAPTER THIRTY-NINE

Angela gently closed the door then faced the bathroom mirror and released a silent scream.

She loved this man.

She loved him so much it hurt.

She gripped the corners of the vanity. What was wrong with his family? It was bad enough that they lacked a sense of humor. But they lacked compassion too? She couldn't imagine Damon as a sick little boy with no one to turn to. Pretending that he was well, when he was not.

Damon would do that, being a person who was so eager to appear he had everything figured out. He'd hide any ailments and suffer alone. Angela briefly shut her eyes against tears, thinking of the lonely little boy he'd once been.

It had been different for her. She couldn't afford to be sick. Her mother taking time off work meant less food in the fridge or a missed electric bill. But her mother never made her feel that she didn't care. Her mother would make Angela food to heat up when she could. Whenever she was sick, her mother would check on her after a long day (twice she'd woken up to the lingering smell of citrus-scented cleaning solution and knew her mother had been there, it became the sweetest scent to her). A mother's care.

But Damon hadn't had that.

Angela took a series of deep, calming breaths. She couldn't be kind and understanding when she was boiling with rage on his behalf. She didn't want to make him feel bad. He loved his family. She knew that and it wasn't her place to judge them. Even though she did.

She found them guilty of some of the most unkind acts known to childhood. She could easily imagine his mother ripping the head off of a beloved teddy bear if Damon had grown too attached in a misguided attempt of toughening him up. She was that kind of woman. That was how she showed her love.

Angela pushed herself away from the vanity. She wasn't supposed to care this much. Caring this much was dangerous. Loving him was hard enough, but loving was easier. One could love an object or a person from a distance.

Caring was much more intimate. With care came responsibility and worry and the desire to protect. And she told herself she didn't want that. But that was a lie. The moment she'd made him her lover she'd shattered any chance of being detached.

She'd told him to trust her and she wouldn't let him regret it.

He'd asked for a favor, he'd revealed something deeply personal about himself. She couldn't ignore that. She also couldn't ignore that she already had grown too attached to him. There was no turning back now. Any moment she had with him had become special and precious. She didn't want to waste it on anger or resentment.

She had to go back in there and not reveal how she felt—whether it was anger or how much he meant to her.

Renewed and determined, Angela left the bathroom and returned to his bedside.

His breathing was soft. He'd fallen asleep. That was a win. She sat down on the bed and pulled the blankets up again, she didn't know why they seemed to keep falling down. However, that was nothing to complain about. The sight of his bare chest was a welcomed one.

One she missed. She wished she was pulling the blankets down instead. Inhaling the heady scent of his skin, the delicious sensation of his hard body on top of hers, his hot breath against her neck.

She wanted to slip her hand underneath the blanket and sweep her hand over the muscles of his stomach and then his thighs. Oh those thighs...beautiful thick thighs that made her mouth go dry with longing. She wanted to slide into the bed beside him and hold him close and press her lips over every inch of him and let him know how treasured he was. But she wouldn't.

She stood.

Damon grabbed her arm. "You promised me a couple minutes."

She gasped in surprise. "You're awake."

He opened his eyes. "Of course I am. You think I'd miss this." He tugged her back down. "I was afraid I'd scared you away."

"Impossible. Why would you think that?"

"It's a corny request."

"It's a sweet one."

Damon bit his lip before he shook his head. "You don't think so."

"Yes, I do."

His gaze turned neutral—distant, but a note of worry entered his tone. "I can see it on your face. You don't like being a caretaker."

"I do actually. This is a practice run for when Jadin's older and I have to do this for him."

Damon shook his head again. "You're lying."

"What if I am?"

He began to sit up. "Tell me what's on your mind."

Angela gently pushed him back down. "I can't."

"Why not?"

"Because it's about your mother, your father and the rest of your family. I am thinking very horrible things right now and comparing them to animals and stinky things you'd rather not know about."

Worry left his gaze replaced with amusement and relief. "I see."

"So now you understand?"

His expression softened with tenderness. "You're angry on my behalf."

"Try livid."

He took her hand. "Don't be. This moment makes up for all of it."

"I wish I could make you smile. You rarely smile with me and it only seems to be when you're with Jadin."

He squeezed her hand. "Who cares about making me smile, when you make me happy?"

Her mood lifted. "Do you want me to hum you a song?"

He grimaced. "I've heard you in the shower, your singing is even worse than your cooking."

She narrowed her eyes and said in a threatening tone,

"You're lucky you're sick right now, but I'm going to get you for that later."

He closed his eyes unafraid. "I look forward to that," he said. "Read me something."

Angela looked around the room. "You don't have any books."

He motioned to his side table. "Yes, I do."

She saw a white colored device as thin as a magazine with a large screen and a small keypad. "What is that?"

"It's my e-reader. Basically an iPod for books. It can hold about fifteen hundred. It's a wave of the future."

Angela picked up the device and started going through its content.

When a minute passed Damon said, "What are you doing?"

"I'm trying to find something to read to you. None of these books will do."

"You can buy something new like you would online. Here," he said showing her the feature on the device.

Angela nodded in satisfaction. "That's better."

He tried to peer over her shoulder. "What exactly are you looking for?"

She turned her back to him. "Give me a minute. Yes. This is it." She adjusted his pillow then gently pushed him back. "Lie down."

"What kind of book is it?"

"You'll see. Here we go. Chapter One." She paused for dramatic effect. "The Cyclone," she said then began reading *The Wonderful Wizard of Oz*.

CHAPTER FORTY

Sometimes Damon wondered if he worked for Ray or if Ray worked for him.

It had been two days since he'd recovered from his last set of spasms and he calmly sat in his study and listened to Ray telling him everything about the household, including the upcoming birthday party for Jadin to celebrate his first year, as if nothing had happened. He didn't look apologetic or concerned.

Once Ray had finished speaking, Damon rested his chin in his hand and said, "You told Angela about the room."

Ray nodded. "Showed her too." He folded his arms, defiant. "Are you going to thank me or give me a bonus?"

Damon folded his arms too. "I should reprimand you."

"You're too smart to waste your time."

Damon let his arms fall. "You're right." He sighed. "How did you know I needed that?"

"Indigenous wisdom."

Damon laughed. "Shut up."

Ray stood. "It's clear you belong together. I wasn't going to let your stupidity keep you apart."

"You just lost your chance for a bonus."

Ray opened the door before he turned to Damon and flashed a wide grin. "No, I didn't. Angela already promised me one."

And Ray deserved it. The birthday party he helped put together was better than either Angela or Damon could have hoped for. In the dining room was a photo garland of autumn leaves highlighting every month of Jadin's life; a circus cake that matched the decorated high chair and party hats.

His mother, Jeannie, complained of the extravagance, and looked annoyed when Damon mentioned wishing his grandfather was there. His father looked bored, but his father always looked bored, Damon had inherited his father's dark coloring and chiseled features, which made it hard to read his face. Angela's friend, Serena, couldn't get enough of the food, Vanessa kept casting nervous glances at Jeannie who had twice asked her if she was seeing anyone since her 'breakup' with Damon and suggested someone she might like to meet.

Megan arrived with her mother, focusing more on tidying her mother's cropped grey hair than anything else for some reason (he had a suspicion it was a wig, but he wasn't sure). Damon felt pleased to finally meet Angela's mother in person since he'd only once spoken to her over the phone. Angela had taken Jadin to visit her mother on a number of occasions but had made it clear she'd preferred he didn't accompany her for one reason or another. Elma Mae Watkins was a pleasant woman who he instantly liked although she couldn't say the same. He'd overheard her in the kitchen talking to Angela saying, "I can't believe you dumped poor Ronald for that. He's decent enough, but he's rather morbid, isn't he?"

"I don't think that's the right term, Mum," Megan said.

"He's not morbid," Angela added.

"So serious looking," their mother said. "It's a party and he doesn't smile. I preferred Ronald. He always had a smile on his face. So handsome."

"Damon's handsome too."

"And wealthier," Megan said.

"Money isn't everything," their mother said.

"Mum, I didn't marry him for his money," Angela said. "He's a wonderful man and very nice to know once you give him a chance."

"I just wished he looked friendlier."

Damon couldn't blame her for her assessment. His family was hardly the jovial type.

Helen looked as miserable as ever and he wondered if his mother had forced her to come. She only briefly softened when Ray said something to her before he addressed the caterer, but it was Leo who worried him the most.

He looked strained and unhappy. When most of the festivities had started to wind down Damon found his brother sitting alone in the formal living room.

"Joyce couldn't make it," he said like a programmed robot.

"I'm not here to ask you about Joyce."

"You're the only one. First it was Mom, then Helen, even Dad." He rubbed his eyes and yawned.

"Are you okay? You look like you haven't slept."

"You're right. I haven't slept in days. I'm afraid to close my eyes."

"Why?"

He yawned again. "I think it's been a week now."

"What happened?"

"I'm getting married. I asked Joyce to wait until after Jadin's party to announce it, so you're the first to know."

Damon hesitated. "I'm not sure if I should offer you congratulations or condolences."

Leo shrugged. "Doesn't matter."

"When's the big day?"

"Next year. July, I think."

"You don't sound too thrilled."

"I uh...tried to break up with Joyce but she wouldn't have it."

Damon's brows shot up. "Joyce won't let you?"

"She's not as harmless as she looks."

"If you love her—"

"Right now she terrifies me. If profuse sweating and pounding heartbeats are signs of love then I've fallen hard."

"Why did you want to break up with her?"

"It was your idea."

Damon stared at him stunned. "How was it my idea?"

"You told me I wasn't being fair. That I should let her go."

"It was a suggestion. I've said it before and you didn't listen."

"It's different now."

"Why?"

"Because Angela said it too and you're different because of her. I've never seen you this happy before. I thought you were crazy to marry the way you did, but you've never seemed more alive. That decision changed you. I don't want to live my life just following our parents' dictates. I wanted to try something different. Be on my own a while. But that's not going to happen."

"You could tell her you need space."

"You can tell her. Remember when you once got a jam

smudge on Helen's history report and she put chewed gum inside your shoes?"

Damon stroked his chin, pensive. "I still have to get her back for that."

"Joyce could think of something worse."

"Couldn't be that bad."

"She threatened to use Mom."

Damon winced. "It's been great knowing you."

Leo pulled something from inside his jacket and handed Damon an envelope.

"What is this?"

"A wedding invitation. One of the five types of invites she's working on. Samples, she calls them. She said she wanted my opinion, but I don't believe her. She's serious about this."

"She may be serious, but if you're not, you can still—"

"I'd no sooner be able to stop a freight train."

Damon studied the linen finish paper invitation then handed it back to Leo. "You can't go through with this. You're going to be miserable."

"I'm sure everything will return to normal after we're married."

"That's a joke, right?"

"Okay, let me rephrase it. I *hope* everything will return to normal after we're married."

"You're deluding yourself. Say goodbye to your bachelor pad, your freedom, the life you once knew. It will all be in the rearview mirror."

"You married Angela."

"That was different. First of all I wanted to marry her."

"How did you know?"

I was desperate and didn't want to be alone. I wanted to help her. But those were not reasons he could share. Plus they weren't entirely true. He could have asked a number of women to marry him for the time he had left. "It felt right. Comfortable. Natural. It wasn't earth shattering or anything, but I just knew that I'd never get bored waking up to her every morning."

"And she doesn't want to change you?"

"No."

"You got lucky. I didn't think a woman like that existed." He tucked the invitation away. "You're the best man of course."

"Better come up with a second choice in case I'm not there."

"Why wouldn't you be there?"

Damon hesitated. He hadn't meant to say that. "No reason."

Leo leaned forward, his gaze sharpened. "Is there something you're not telling me?"

Damon suddenly felt arms wrap around his neck, and was engulfed in a fruity floral scent before someone placed an affectionate kiss on his cheek. "What are you two talking about?" Angela said.

Damon felt his entire body go still. He hadn't been around his family enough to get used to her playacting the doting wife. Every time she did, she caught him off-guard.

"You look so serious." She sat down beside Damon, taking his hand in hers. The firm, warm touch of her hand wasn't only a welcome sensation it was a healing balm, reminding him he wasn't alone. "In case the balloons weren't enough of a sign, this is a party not a funeral."

"I'm getting married," Leo said with all the jubilation of an undertaker.

"Oh." She glanced at Damon. "Am I interrupting—?"

Damon released her hand and rested his arm around her shoulders, bringing her closer to him. When she snuggled even closer like an eager kitten, he had to bite back a moan of pleasure. In the distance he heard Jadin's delighted nonsensical baby babbling and knew if he died at that moment he'd be a happy man.

"Not at all," he told her before he placed a kiss on her forehead then shot his brother a silent look that said, "This is what happiness looks like."

Leo frowned and replied with a look that said, "Easy for you," and Damon replied with a slight shrug and a narrowing of his gaze that said, "End it with Joyce or you'll regret it."

Leo sent Angela a considering look before their father called him to ask his advice on a certain investment. Damon watched his brother leave, for the first time seeing how burdened he looked. Leo always followed the path chosen for him, but now Damon wondered about the price his brother was willing to pay.

CHAPTER FORTY-ONE

*T*his was real.

Damon gathered Angela close that night reveling in the sound of her soft, sweet moans; the arch of her body driving him deeper inside her, letting his erection melt into the hot liquid fire between her thighs while the smooth curve of her body pressed against his.

This was a price he was willing to pay for his deception.

She didn't love him, although she pretended she did.

His family didn't know he was dying.

The little boy he'd grown to love wouldn't remember him.

But this moment was real. Her hands skimming the expanse of his back, the touch and taste of her lips, the way she whispered his name left him breathless. This was real.

"Damon, are you okay?"

He briefly closed his eyes. He hated that question, especially when he wasn't. "Yes," he snapped.

"You're breathing funny."

He swallowed hard and took a deep breath, he didn't have the stamina he'd had before but didn't want to admit it. It embarrassed him that she'd noticed. "I'm fine," he said and kissed her before she could argue. He wouldn't let his illness steal this from him, these moments with her were one of the last things he was willing to let go. He didn't care how much effort it took or how much he had to hide.

Angela was also hiding something. An insatiable hunger. She couldn't get enough of him. She was wearing him out. As if making love to him would lengthen his life. As if she could infuse his life force with hers. She fought back hot tears of rage.

Please don't die. Please don't leave me.

But it was selfish and she knew how much effort each encounter stole from him. His breathing was different and he'd lost weight. Not enough for anyone to notice yet, but it wouldn't be long before there were questions.

And there would be more lies to tell.

His every touch made her senses spin, heightening not only her awareness of him, but the soft, supple ash colored sheets against her body, the glow of the lamplight, the scent of sugar, which reminded her of the rich, moist chocolate birthday cake, she'd gotten to playfully feed him.

But she couldn't be selfish, she had to think of him and not push him to his breaking point.

Angela released her hold on him and dramatically fell back on the bed. "You're wearing me out."

Damon chuckled with masculine pleasure and her heart lifted that he'd fallen for her lie. "That's my goal," he said before he disappeared into the bathroom.

She shifted to the side and gathered the sheets up to her chest, her heart pounding so fast it almost hurt. Every moment he was away from her she worried. Even though it had never happened, she worried about him getting dizzy and collapsing in the bathroom or stumbling and losing his balance. What if he hit his head on the sink? There could be so much blood or worse he could...

"What's wrong?" Damon said in a sharp voice. He stood in the bathroom doorway, naked and beautiful.

Angela forced a nervous laugh. "Why would anything be wrong?"

He walked towards the bed. "You look terrified."

Because the thought of losing you terrifies me. Her gaze swept over him. He looked fine. His face looked a little drawn but overall he looked good. "I'm not. Unless you want a round two, which I don't think I can do."

He slid into the bed beside her. "You're in luck," he said wearily amused. "I don't think I can either."

She heard him sigh and saw his eyes drift close, but she didn't want the night to end yet. She wanted every moment with him to last as long as it could. She shifted closer to him and rested her hand on his shoulder. "What were you and Leo talking about at the party?"

He shook his head. "You don't want to know."

"Yes, I do."

Damon sent her a considering look before he rested against the headboard and told her about Joyce. Angela only partially listened to the outrageous story, taking more interest in the concern in Damon's voice and the worry that had darkened his eyes. After he'd finished speaking, she gave his arm a reassuring squeeze and said, "I think she's just upset, I don't think she means it."

"I think she does."

"She wouldn't want to force a man to marry her."

Damon sniffed. "You haven't met her. I can't believe you met with my brother and didn't tell me."

"I did, but you'd disappeared to your secret room, remember? I sent you a text."

He nodded. "True. I'd returned from Manila after appearing as a guest chef on a show there. It was thrilling and grueling and I wasn't sure I'd make it but it was fun to be inside a kitchen again."

"And you exhausted yourself."

"Hmm." He kissed her before he slid underneath the sheets and turned his back to her. "'Night."

"When are you going to cook for me?" she asked in a soft voice.

Angela sensed rather than felt him stiffen. The room wasn't dark, but the glow of the lights seemed to dim, the air crackled with a tense silence.

But she wouldn't let his silence frighten her. "All these months and you haven't even boiled an egg."

"I don't cook for family."

"Never?"

He faced her, his dark eyes met hers. "Never."

"Why not?"

"Because." He moved his shoulders in an impatient shrug. "It doesn't matter. I hired a chef more for my family than myself. It's better that way."

"Well, I'm not really family."

His brows shot up. "You're my wife."

"Not really."

His tone hardened with a steel edge. "Yes. Really."

Angela blinked, a shiver of unease coursing through her. His voice had the warning of a rattlesnake. She was entering dangerous territory, but she felt it was an important chasm to cross. "Okay, let me put it a different way. I'm the family you chose, not the family you were given so can't you make an exception?"

He hesitated. She sensed his vulnerability. She lightly touched his cheek.

"Even when I worked with you I never had a chance to try your cooking. Please. It doesn't have to be something fancy."

Damon turned away from her and mumbled, "All right."

Her heart soared with joy. *Success!* She kissed his cheek. "Great. Breakfast, lunch, dinner or appetizer?"

"It'll be a surprise."

CHAPTER FORTY-TWO

She hadn't been looking forward to this kind of surprise.

But she couldn't look disappointed.

Even though she was.

When Damon had called her to dinner that Saturday, Angela had eagerly left Jadin with the nanny expecting a breathtaking feast.

Instead she sat under the crystal chandelier of their formal dining room and stared at a simple dish of red beans and rice and chicken.

She doubted he'd put any effort into the meal. The chicken looked curried, perhaps that was something. Or was this his tiny rebellion for suggesting that he cook for her?

Angela lifted her eyes and met Damon's dark assessing gaze. He stood on the other side of the table with his arms folded, his face neutral. But his eyes were not.

His eyes were of a man who'd made others break out in a sweat. This was a test. A challenge. Demon Damon was in attendance, she could feel the heat level rise in the room. The stakes were high.

She pointed at him. "I told you that expression is dangerous."

He shrugged. "I can't help how I look."

"You can when someone is trying to eat. You're making me nervous."

His hands fell to his hips. "You're stalling."

She was. She didn't want to pretend that she'd enjoyed such a plain ordinary meal, but she would. She lifted the fork resigned. It didn't matter that he'd served the dish in the elegant dining room and placed it on crisp white china with a polished platinum edge. Nothing could make the dish itself remarkable.

Served her right for expecting more. Angela took a bite then stopped.

She'd had red beans and rice plenty of times in her life, but nothing like this.

She felt her senses explode with bursts of pleasure. This was extraordinary.

She'd never had such fluffy rice float over her tongue, mingled with red beans that kept the rice from feeling as if it would float away. And then the chicken. The curry spice should have overwhelmed the overall flavor but seemed to make the rice and beans burst into an extra-savory creation. Demon Damon had taken a simple meal and touched it with the uncanny magic of the gods. She took several more bites before she stared at him stunned.

"What did you do?" she asked him.

"I boiled the rice with sweet coconut milk for added flavor."

"You did more than that."

He winked. "A chef's secret."

She motioned to a chair. "Sit down. You've got to have some of this."

Damon sat down in front of her and shook his head. "No, I'm fine." He rested his chin in his hand and watched her, a warm glow of joy washing over him, easing the tension that had kept him hostage.

The surprised delight on her face made all the anxiety and doubt that had seized him as he put the meal together worth it. He'd boiled the rice and cooked the chicken, fighting his hardest to forget his family's dismissal of his efforts and his close relationship with his grandfather. Food had become too special to share with anyone close. It revealed too much of him. He could entertain and delight a stranger, but had never managed to do the same for anyone he cared about. He hadn't been sure he'd succeed.

The sound of her fork lightly scraping against the plate as she scooped up another mouthful of rice was like music to him. He heard Angela sniff and saw tears streaming down her face. "Thank you," she said in a choked voice.

Damon swallowed and fought back his own tears.

She truly understood what this meal meant to him.

He felt his life come full circle. Finally he could share his love of food with someone he loved. This meal would be something she'd always remember. It was one of his final gifts to her.

He'd been redeemed.

He accepted his fate.

He had all that he wanted.

Then two days before Christmas he received the worst news of his life.

CHAPTER FORTY-THREE

"*I*t's not terminal."

An emergency. That's what the doctor had told him.

Vanessa had pestered him into seeing another specialist after his lethargy and weight loss had become more noticeable, but after another series of test he'd become resigned that time was running out and there was nothing anyone could do.

His fourth—or was it his fifth (he'd lost track)— doctor had left an urgent message telling Damon to schedule an appointment.

He now sat in the examining room, glad for once that he wasn't in a hospital gown or getting blood drawn, but wondering why his life felt as if it had been upended again.

The doctor, a silver haired woman with a gummy grin, was talking but he could only process some of the words.

Previous doctor...thought it was cancer...something else... rare...still a concern...be vigilant...a type of fungus.

Damon held up his hands, feeling disoriented. "Stop. Say that again."

The doctor blinked. "What do you need me to repeat?"

Everything. "It isn't cancer?"

"No, it's a fungus. You'll need surgery to remove most of it and the remainder can be addressed with other less radical treatment."

Damon paused. Was it possible to feel as if one had been punched, dropped and wrung out to dry at the same time? "What are you saying? I'm not going to die?"

The doctor beamed. "No, you've been given a second chance at life. Now, there are possible side effects to this procedure. It's possible you'll lose your sense of smell and taste."

"For a while?"

"Permanently."

"You find that a minor consequence?" Damon scoffed. "Do you know what I do for a living? I'm a chef. My senses are everything."

"You're getting your life back. This will be the price you pay."

She made it sound so simple, but he could take losing a limb over this new prognosis. Food was his life. He'd have to spend the rest of it without enjoying the savory smells of sweet mangos and spices, the creamy taste of melted butter on toast. What was he without those things? He might as well be dead.

"What if I don't have the surgery?"

She looked at him surprised then sputtered, "Well then the fungus could continue to spread."

"What about medication?"

"It's too virulent right now. Medication won't be enough."

"It'll have to be."

"You need to think this through."

"But it's just a fungus. It's not malignant, right? It won't kill me."

"Unchecked it could."

"But not as quickly as when you thought it was cancer."

A flash of irritation crossed her face. "We don't know. We've never had someone who didn't address it once it was discovered." She took a deep breath. "Take time to discuss this with your wife."

His wife. For a brief moment he'd forgotten he had one.

He had a wife. *A wife who expected him to die.*

Damon rubbed his forehead and swore.

"In the meantime let me schedule—"

Damon shook his head. "I'm not having surgery."

"This fungus may sound benign, but it isn't. It could cover your organs even reach your vision and cause blindness."

He could take being blind. At least he could still taste and touch and smell.

But that wasn't his major challenge. It was that he wasn't going to die.

Angela hadn't married him for himself but for what he could provide her and her time with him had come with a deadline. She wouldn't want to spend the rest of her life with him. Let alone with a version of him that wasn't one hundred percent healthy.

Last month, instead of spending Thanksgiving with their families, Damon had treated Angela and Jadin to a trip to Jamaica. He'd wanted to show her where his beloved Popa had lived. He'd taken them around the island, showing them all the places he'd enjoyed as a child, where he'd eaten his beloved oats porridge with chopped pears, and telling her how much Popa had helped make him the man he was today.

On the sun warmed beach, underneath the shade of a large palm tree, feeding Jadin a mango slice, Angela had taken many pictures of them, specifically him, so that Jadin would have something to remember him by. Those were to be a treasure. What would those pictures be worth now?

A suffocating sadness gripped his heart.

If he didn't die he could lose everything he cared about. He dreaded the thought of Angela leaving his life again and she'd take Jadin too.

Dying would have been easier.

What did he tell her?

Did he *have* to tell her?

The holidays were usually the loneliness season for him. He usually came up with a reason to be on the road and provide cheer for others while feeling empty inside. But this time he'd looked forward to it.

Ray had hired a professional team to decorate both the interior and exterior of the house for the holidays. Bright white lights shimmered along the house trim and inside the scent of holly and pine greeted him from the garlands and eight foot Christmas tree. They had coordinated the gift wrapping paper to complement the blue and silver color scheme of the family room and the ornaments on the tree. Large red poinsettias stood on either side of the fireplace where three stockings hung and fuschia-veined blossoms sat among tall white candlesticks on the dining table where he planned to surprise her with a holiday feast.

He couldn't tell her yet.

He couldn't lose her yet.

He'd have to keep this secret until the New Year.

CHAPTER FORTY-FOUR

Damon's headaches were beginning to worry her. They had increased in frequency and intensity.

But Damon wouldn't complain. He'd shrug and say, "That's what painkillers are for," then brush her worry aside. But when it came to his health, there was nothing she was willing to brush aside. Not his loss of appetite, his sometimes labored breathing or the amount of times he'd excused himself from playing with Jadin, although she sensed he wanted to but didn't have the energy.

She knew time was running out. They'd spent a magical Christmas day together. He'd not only surprised her with a blue long sleeve lace slip and a black lace bra and panty set (with a note that said 'this is lingerie') but also a pearl necklace handmade in Peru by a woman-owned ethically sourced company.

They'd greeted the New Year with a dinner of honey-garlic cauliflower, rice and sultry butter chicken, but now it was late January. A blanket of snow had hardened over the trees and bushes, making the branches sag under the weight.

To some the winter white landscape signified something fresh and new, but it left her heart cold. The snow was covering the life underneath it. Just like Damon was covering what his disease was doing to his body.

She wouldn't let him hide. Something felt wrong.

She went to his medicine cabinet, grabbed a bottle, read the label and paused. It was new. When had he changed his medication? Perhaps the headache was a side effect?

The name of this new prescription was very similar to what he had been taking before but had a different dosage. Had the doctor made a mistake? The pharmacy? Was he taking something he shouldn't have? The thought terrified her.

She called the doctor whose name was on the bottle.

"I see that Damon's on this new medication," she said, when the doctor answered, "but it's causing a lot of headaches is there a chance he could get a lower dose?"

"It's the correct dosage."

"Is there a reason why you switched him?"

Her voice was professionally distant. "You'll have to ask him."

"Could you—"

"I was not given consent to reveal anything to you. I'm sorry but you'll have to speak to him."

"But I'm his wife—"

"Like I said," the doctor said with a note of sympathy, "without the patient's written consent there's nothing I can tell you."

Angela disconnected, frustrated. She knew going direct to Damon wouldn't get her the answers she wanted. At first she thought of trying to hack into his cell phone and laptop, then toyed with the idea of eavesdropping on his calls, even bugging them, but decided against it.

It was only through luck that she discovered the truth. She'd put her car in the shop for a tune up and asked to borrow his and had found a wadded up document in the glove compartment when she'd looked for tissues.

She found a detailed document stating a new diagnosis. It described a virulent fungus that was suspected to have come from being exposed to a certain bacteria particular to the waters of the Tasman, Caspian or Caribbean Sea, where Damon had enjoyed swimming most of his childhood. It was an extremely rare disease and often misdiagnosed or overlooked. Many who have the disease don't have symptoms, but those who do, have various outlooks depending on the level of organ damage at the time of the diagnosis.

Angela let her gaze skim over the pages of information that helped explain all his experiences and his long suffering. Then her heart stopped. There was no cure, but there was hope. She read a description of a medical procedure.

A surgery.

Angela read the possible outcomes and softly swore. She understood why Damon hadn't told her. It would impact his career, but his life mattered more.

It would be a battle. She expected to win.

CHAPTER FORTY-FIVE

A chill.

He felt a chill.

A chill like when your teacher catches you putting a frog in your backpack, or your mother catches you smashing cookies so that you can sprinkle them over your broccoli, saying you thought they would improve the taste.

Or the time you got caught in the shower when the husband of the woman you'd been seeing (you hadn't known she was married) arrived with his girlfriend (who she didn't know about) and they both started comparing notes on who was the better cheater (you remember that had been a very bad day).

It was that kind of chill and Damon felt it the moment Angela walked into the kitchen. He'd been enjoying a nice afternoon snack and knew it wouldn't end well.

First, the way she walked into the room was a sign. She looked determined. She never entered a kitchen determined. She liked to avoid them, unless offered food or to work, she sped in them and quickly exited.

No, she had come into the kitchen with a mission. He swallowed. He really hoped she hadn't found a new recipe she wanted them to try together. He wasn't in the mood.

"Before you say anything," he told her. "The dinner schedule for this week has already been decided."

She sat down. "Good."

He waited.

She stared.

He swallowed again. She didn't just look determined, she looked mad. He hadn't noticed that before. If he'd done anything wrong, she'd have to tell him. He wasn't one to play guessing games. He was a man who knew patience. A good chef knew the importance of timing.

She put a medicine bottle on the table. "I think these might be causing your headaches."

"Hm." Was that all? She was worried about him? He felt himself relax. "Maybe, I'll get used to it."

"You prefer headaches to surgery?"

He met her gaze and the chill turned to panic. She knew. How could she have found out? "Relax, it's no big deal. My body will adjust."

"The doctor isn't so sure. Why didn't you tell me about this? You switch medication, turn down surgery, you're—"

"Not going to die," he finished because she didn't seem to be able to.

She folded her arms. "When were you going to tell me?"

He sat back and sighed. "At first I was planning to wait until after Christmas. And then I thought I'd wait until New Years. But after New Year's Day there's Valentine's Day—"

"So you were never going to tell me?" she asked in a quiet voice. A too quiet voice that he couldn't read.

"I would have eventually."

"What would you say?"

"I'd tell you that you didn't have to stay married to me any longer, but that I'd still like you to be a part of my life."

"And after that?"

Damon threw up his hands exasperated. "What are you expecting? A five year plan? I didn't think that far ahead. I wasn't trying to deceive you. I just like having you in my life too much to risk losing you. I wouldn't pretend to die or anything. I'm sorry I worried you. It wasn't my intention. But now you know that things are okay and—"

Angela pounded the table. "Don't lie to me."

"I'm not lying," he said startled by her outburst. "I'm telling you the truth."

"You may not die this year. But this fungus could eventually mutate and kill you."

"In a decade or two. They don't know enough about it, but it's manageable."

"You don't know that. But surgery—"

He shook his head. "Is out of the question."

"So it's really a lie then."

"What is?"

"That you want to be with Jadin and me. You'd prefer to let this thing ravage your body than take the steps to live a fully functioning life."

His voice cracked in disbelief. "Fully functioning? Is that a joke? Do you know what I'd lose if I lost those senses? How can I be an instructor? All those ideas of me being a private teacher to help raise funds for the DRCA program would disappear. How about experimenting with new recipes? I'd rather die than be a shell of my former self. Don't ask me to do that. Please."

"You're more than what you do. And what if you don't lose

your senses? There's a twenty percent chance nothing will change. Or that it might be brief. You have so much life to live."

Damon shook his head, adamant. "You didn't sign up for this. You thought I was going to die."

"And I'm glad that you're not. I'm glad that I get to have a future with you because that's what I want." She took his hand. "I'm not going anywhere. We'll face this together..." She let her words fade away when he shook his head. She took a deep breath. "Please."

It was a risk. What if she didn't stay? What if he took this chance and if he couldn't maintain his business and—

"This will not sink us," Angela said. "Your business and brand are solid. Without realizing it by making plans as if you were dying, you put everything on a solid foundation to outlast you. Plus, I will make sure that the DRCA outlasts us."

He knew she was trying to reassure him, but he wasn't really worried about the business. He was worried about what he could offer. The kind of man he'd be after this. Food was his life. What would he be without it?

"Trust me."

He did, but not about this. He pulled his hand away. She was asking him to give up much more than what had been his passion. She was also asking him to give up what made him happy like the scent of coconut and baby oil, her shower soaked skin, the taste of her mouth.

His true fear was coming true. He'd started to depend on her. Need her. It frightened him. What if this was just the beginning of something worse?

Without his skill he'd be ordinary. His culinary skills were what had always differentiated them. She may be a brilliant marketer, business woman but he was the one with artistic skill. He could work magic in the kitchen.

But with one cut of the knife that could be taken away. She'd been in awe of his talent. What would he have to offer her after that? What would he do when he couldn't make sure that the chocolate covered strawberries were up to standard?

What if his life was reduced to the fact that he wasn't able to tell the difference between fresh carrots and canned ones? Frozen versus freezer burned?

He folded his arms. "I'm sorry. But I've made up my mind. You have to accept me as I am and the choices I need to make for myself."

"Damon, let's talk—"

"There's nothing more to talk about. I'm not having surgery. That's final. It's my life, not yours."

Angela surged to her feet. "You're right. Since I'm not your *real* wife, we don't have a life together. You can keep yours." She turned. "I'll pack my things."

"There's no reason to leave. The house is big enough for both of us and you know I don't want you to go."

She took a deep breath and he feared she'd tell him she was leaving anyway. "Okay, I'll just move back to my old room."

"I don't want you to do that either."

"What do you want me to do?"

He walked over to her, his voice tender. "Nothing. I want to keep things as they are. I want to save the life I have. I still want you in it. As me. Please understand that."

She took a step back. "I don't. I'll start looking for a new place."

"Angela—"

She glared at him with hot tears, filling her eyes. "As I told you before I'll stand by your side for a lot of things, but I won't stand around and watch you kill yourself."

CHAPTER FORTY-SIX

She had to leave.

She didn't want to leave, but she had to. She couldn't stand around and do nothing. She'd kept his secret for him, but no more. She wanted to stop pretending. She no longer wanted to act as if everything was all right when it wasn't.

Angela sat on the edge of her bed and squeezed her eyes closed but it didn't stop her from seeing the devastated look on Damon's face when she'd told him she would leave. She couldn't shut out the quiet, pleading tone in his voice when he'd asked permission to visit Jadin after she'd gone.

Her closed eyes couldn't stop the tears or drown out the memory of him promising her that he'd always provide for Jadin and that she could keep her job at the DRCA program.

She opened her eyes and wiped away her tears. She didn't want his money. She wanted him healthy. Surgery may not be a cure but at least he'd be healthier than he was now. Why couldn't he see that?

Anger burned so bright within her that she couldn't sleep

that night and the following day she decided it was best she left the house as soon as possible. There were too many memories of them together—playing with Jadin in the nursery, the scent of something warm and delicious shimmering on the stove that he wanted her to taste, the sound of his footsteps when he returned from a trip and the hug he gave her when she greeted him.

The grand house also held the echo of lost possibilities. He was throwing away a new life they could share, that hurt the most. So she had to escape in order to clear her thoughts.

But ending up at Megan's house turned out to be a mistake.

"Bye-bye," Jadin said in greeting, his favorite and only word.

"I knew you'd break his heart," Megan said, removing Jadin's winter coat while Angela pulled off her slush covered boots in the foyer.

Angela stared at her sister outraged. "He broke mine first. I want him well, how is that wrong?"

Megan hung up Jadin's coat before she carried him into the living room.

Angela raced after her. "Are you ignoring me?"

She took a seat, setting Jadin on her lap. "I told you he loves you."

"If that were true he'd take the risk to—"

"Prove that he loves you?" Megan said in a sour tone. Jadin squirmed in her lap so she set him on the ground, where he started to explore.

"That's not fair." Angela said, snatching a glass figurine from Jadin's grasp that he'd grabbed from a side table. Her sister's stylish home was not child-proof.

Jadin gasped in surprise then his chin trembled in frustration before he sat back and started to cry.

"Do you want to know what's not fair?" Megan said over her nephew's wails. "You pretending not to know how much you're hurting him."

Angela scooped Jadin up and stroked his back, feeling her patience thinning. "I'm not pretending. For the first time in months I'm being completely honest. You keep talking about him, but what about me?" Angela stomped her foot; Jadin continued to cry. "Do you think it was easy to leave? Do you think I want to separate him from Jadin? I desperately want him to live." Her voice shook. "He didn't even give me a chance to celebrate that. Instead, he lied to me and then he does this." She left the living room and unzipped one of the suitcases she'd left in the hallway. She dug inside until she found Jadin's favorite toy—a stuffed ice cream cone, that annoyingly smelled like Damon—and handed it to him. Jadin blinked then hiccupped before he accepted it from her.

Relieved, she returned to the living room where Megan sat with her arms now folded.

"Does what?" she said.

Angela placed Jadin on the couch before she sat down beside him. "Huh?"

"You said 'he does this'. What exactly is he doing?"

"He's pretending things aren't as bad as they seem. I know he did it as a child because he had to, but he's a man now. He has a responsibility to take care of himself. But he won't and I can't—" She shook her head. "No, I *refuse* to watch the man I care about suffer. I did it for all these months, marrying him because he was dying. I felt sorry for him. I'm not pretending anymore."

Megan sent her a curious look. "I thought you married him because you loved him."

Angela paused—caught. "It's complicated."

"Either you love someone or you don't. That's not complicated to me." She stood.

"Bye-bye," Jadin said.

Megan shook her head before she left the room, leaving Angela feeling even more alone than before.

CHAPTER FORTY-SEVEN

*A*ngela lasted two days at her sister's house before she decided a hotel was a little more peaceful and a lot less infuriating.

She set Jadin's stroller in the corner and began unpacking their things.

A quiet hotel room didn't ask her about the financial repercussions of her breakup or even the parental arrangement she'd have to agree to.

A quiet hotel room wouldn't judge her. It would leave her alone to think.

Angela closed her suitcase, only half-way unpacked, and sat on the bed feeling drained.

She had to come up with a new plan. She was on her own again. She had to depend on herself. She couldn't trust her life and her son's life to a man who wouldn't be responsible enough to look after himself. One who was being so stubborn and selfish? Ronald had been stubborn and selfish enough for her. She wasn't falling into that trap again, placating and accommodating a man who only cared about himself. His needs. His wants.

If Damon really cared about them he'd do whatever it took to stay alive and well.

Megan was wrong. Damon didn't love them. Their marriage was a lie.

If only her love for him was a lie too.

Angela stood ready to start unpacking again, but stopped when she heard someone knock on the door.

Her pulse quickened. Who could it be? Megan? Damon?

She looked through the peephole but could only see the back of a man's head. She swung the door open.

Leo turned around with a silly grin on his face, his right eye swollen shut.

Angela stared at him shocked. "What happened to you?"

"The good news is I'm not getting married."

He stumbled inside and closed the door behind him.

"Joyce punched you?"

He pointed to his eye. "No, this was Damon." He opened his jacket, lifted up his maroon sweater and showed her a bruise on his side. "This was Joyce."

"Why would Damon punch you?"

"Because I made him mad."

Angela sniffed the air when he walked passed her. "Have you been drinking?"

"A little, but I'm only drunk on happiness."

"How did you find me?"

"Your sister. The mean one."

"I only have one sister."

"Yeah, that's the one. She told me where you were." Leo walked over to Jadin, who was sitting in his stroller and tickled the baby's cheek. "Hey there," he said and Jadin said, "Bye-

Bye," before Leo straightened and looked around the hotel room perplexed. "This is awfully small. You could have at least gotten a suite."

The hotel was far from one of the pricier choices available downtown, but with its soothing gray and white colors and plush wall-to-wall carpeting it was far from shabby. She wanted to live on her salary and not the lifestyle she'd grown used to with Damon. "This is fine. What are you doing here?"

He sat on one of the beds. "You got a double, why didn't you get a king size at least?"

"Leo, what are you doing here?"

"I wanted to talk to you."

"First we need to get something for that eye."

"Relax, it's no big deal."

Angela's patience snapped. "That's what Damon says! What is it with you and your family? Why do you pretend things are better than they are? You can hardly see out of that eye. It's completely discolored and—"

"Did Damon ever tell you about Popa?"

Angela stopped, surprised by the change of topic. "Yes, of course. Everyone who knows him knows about his beloved Popa. I can't count the number of times he's told me about his beloved oats porridge."

"Served with chopped pears," Leo added.

"Of course," Angela said with a laugh, a little shocked that she still could. "He told me everything about him. We even visited Jamaica so Damon could show me where Popa used to live. He also told me lots of stories of Popa's rise in the culinary world."

"Did he tell you Popa was really a 'she'?"

Angela sat down in front of him and narrowed her eyes. "Are you sure you're not drunk?"

Leo met her gaze, his voice firm. "I'm not drunk."

"Your grand*father* was a woman?"

Leo nodded. "The Remeer side of my family is used to keeping secrets. It's how we survive. Popa had no choice really. When she was growing up there weren't many viable opportunities for a girl who had ambition and wanted to provide for her family. She discovered striking out on her own as a woman was much more dangerous than for a man. So she left her birthplace of Antigua as a woman and arrived in Jamaica as a man. She applied for a job at a restaurant as a dishwasher using a new identity—Damon Reemer.

"He made his way up from there. In his mid-twenties he met a young woman whose man had abandoned her and left her with two young children. That was our grandmother."

"Did she know that—"

Leo nodded. "Yes and she didn't care." He sniffed. "I wouldn't be surprised if she preferred it. She only twice mentioned her first husband to me and said he was a useless as shoes on a chicken. They had a happy union. I don't know how they managed it, but my mother didn't discover the truth until after Popa retired. When she did it bothered her. She was ashamed of the deception and Popa's life choices. She couldn't understand it."

Leo sighed. "Damon's attachment to Popa frightened her. What you have to understand is that Damon not only loved Popa because of who he was, but because he'd had the courage to carve out the life he wanted to live despite all the challenges. Damon always admired that and that's what scared our parents.

"Our mother especially wanted to be more normal than normal. But Damon has always had to live life on his own terms. That's how he feels truly free and most himself.

Wanting him to be something different means you don't know him at all."

Angela looked at Leo's swollen eye. "Why did he punch you?"

"Because I punched him first."

She blinked, surprised. She could hardly imagine Leo swatting a fly, let alone throwing a punch. "I don't believe you."

"It's true. I came by the house to tell him I'd finally broken up with Joyce and he told me you'd left him and taken Jadin and then he told me why—"

Leo paused and took a deep breath, anger clouding his features. "He'd told me that he'd thought he was dying and that was why he'd gotten married. That it was all a sham."

"And you punched him because he betrayed you?"

"No, I punched him because he was lying to me again. I knew he married you because he'd always loved you and he always will. And then I told him I quit."

Angela shook her head. "You're falling for his lie too. It was all make-believe, don't you get it?"

"You don't get it," Leo said in a hard voice that for a moment made her a little afraid of him. He tapped his thumbs together and softened his tone as if sensing her unease. "You once told me I needed courage. I'm now telling you the same. But you'll have to accept two things first."

Angela frowned. "Two things?"

"Yes. You'll have to accept that he loves you. Second you'll have to accept my brother as he is, not how you want him to be."

Angela turned to look at Jadin who had fallen asleep, his head tilted to the side. Tear filled her eyes as the sight of him reminded her of another moment in late summer when she'd found both Jadin and Damon asleep on the couch in the family room. The high pitched sounds of a kid's cartoon played on the TV. Jadin had been a little smaller then, but he'd fallen asleep in the same position on Damon's lap. Damon had fallen asleep with his head tilted back and she remembered carefully sliding a pillow underneath his head afraid he'd get a crick neck.

But he wasn't completely asleep, he briefly opened his eyes and gazed at her with a look of such tenderness she felt her entire body grow warm. He mouthed, "Thank you," before he closed his eyes again.

Leo doesn't lie. That was one of the things Damon had been certain about his brother. If Leo said Damon loved her that meant it was true.

Damon truly did love her.

But instead of feeling relieved Angela felt frightened and ashamed. The devastation on his face held more significance now. She'd been blind to what Megan and Leo had always seen.

He'd shown her his love in so many ways, but she'd been afraid to accept it. Afraid that if she did, she somehow wouldn't be free. She didn't want to trust and become dependent on something he could take away from her. It had been easier to pretend his love wasn't real, that it had been for show.

Her fear had caused her to hurt him when he'd needed her the most. She'd let him down.

She hung her head. "I don't know how to go back."

"That's okay." He held out a handkerchief.

She took the patterned cotton item from him then looked up at him amazed. "You actually carry this around with you?"

"Of course," he said, his tone silently adding, "doesn't every man of distinction?"

Angela wiped her eyes suddenly feeling less down than

she did before. Despite his stuffy ways and busted eye, Leo amused her. "Thank you."

"You can thank me by saving my brother from misery. I don't care if you're afraid. Trust me, I was terrified when I faced Joyce and told her I couldn't marry her, but I don't regret it. It was the first time in my life I did something for myself." He sighed. "And I don't know what I'm going to do next, but I'll figure it out." Leo paused. He glanced at Jadin, then out the window, before he shifted his keen gaze to her. "I don't think you saw my brother on that cooking competition and only saw a man who was a potential client. I think you saw a man who was perfect for you."

CHAPTER FORTY-EIGHT

Someone was trying to kill him.

Damon swore then groaned in pain. He had to change his doorbell, why did it always sound like an angry buzzer after a night of drinking. The sound was even worse when his pain medicine started to wear off. Damn, he'd forgotten Leo had a mean swing. Damn tennis.

Damon gently touched around his swollen eye, grateful his brother hadn't aimed for his nose.

"Should I get that?" a soft feminine voice asked next to him.

"It will stop soon," he managed in a hoarse whisper. At least he hoped it would.

Damon wasn't sure what part of his body hurt more, his head or his heart. The sound of the buzzer's angry ring seemed to exacerbate both.

Angela was gone.

Jadin was gone.

He'd even lost Leo.

He'd have to live the remainder of his life a shell of a man.

The buzzing stopped. He sighed in relief. Quiet. Beautiful quiet. This was nice. Now if only he could get back to sleep...

"What is it with you and beautiful women?"

Damon paused. The tone sounded ironic, but it wasn't male so it couldn't belong to Ray or Leo. Helen didn't do irony well and his mother had *never* ventured to his bedroom before (she'd likely choose to shop at a thrift store first). The only woman he could think of...

He sat up and saw Angela standing in the doorway. But she wasn't looking at him. She was looking at the woman who'd fallen back asleep beside him. A woman wearing one of his shirts. The long sleeved white one with thin red stripes that she'd bought him for Christmas.

Shit!

He frantically waved his hands as the events of the previous evening night came flooding back to him. Vanessa had come over in tears, upset over a breakup, and he'd cheered her up with some wine. Maybe too much. At some point she'd gotten sick on herself and he'd given her one of his shirts to wear instead. Right...

Now he remembered...

That's how they'd ended up in his bedroom. They'd both been too lazy to go back downstairs so they'd stayed in his room and talked more then fell asleep. He stared at Angela wondering how he could explain that.

"This is not what you think." He swung his legs over the side of the bed. It took him a moment to realize he only had his black boxers on. When had he taken off his trousers?

He met Angela's gaze. "Nothing happened, I promise you."

Angela folded her arms her expression unreadable. "Uh huh."

He stood. "I—we just—"

"I don't care. Meet you downstairs." She left and closed the door.

Damon pressed a hand against his forehead and swore. This was bad.

"Relax," Vanessa said, her voice muffled by the pillow. "She didn't sound angry."

"You're awake?"

She turned to him. "Of course I'm awake."

"You didn't have to pretend to be asleep."

"It was easier than laughing."

He grabbed a pair of jeans. "It's not funny."

She leaned on her side and rested her head in her hand. She watched him with an amused expression while he struggled with the zipper. "Yes, it is."

He glared at her. "If she thinks—"

"She won't. Hurry up. You shouldn't keep her waiting."

❧

HE COULDN'T FIND HER AT FIRST.

He thought he'd find her in the family room, but when she wasn't there, he went into the formal living room, then the formal dining room. But when she wasn't there either he feared she'd left or perhaps he'd imagined it all.

He should have worked harder to make her stay from the moment she'd found out the truth. He should have fought for her and Jadin and not let them go. This was his punishment.

"She's in the kitchen," Ray calmly told him as he emerged from the study and headed down the hall.

Damon grabbed his arm. "You could have warned me she was here."

Ray yanked his arm free and smoothed out the wrinkles of his shirt sleeve. He sent Damon a bored, tolerant look before he said, "I manage your house, not your life." He turned and continued down the hall.

Damon shook his head once again wondering who was really in charge. But he didn't have time to think about that now.

He rushed into the kitchen and found Angela sitting at the table.

She jumped to her feet when she saw him.

He took a step towards her, wanting to pull her close.

"I'm sorry—," they said in unison.

They paused then both said, "What are you sorry for?"

Angela held up her hand. "Let me go first. Sit down."

Damon took a deep breath but didn't move. "Where's Jadin?"

"Leo's looking after him." She paused. "He told me the truth about Popa."

His stomach clenched with unease. Popa meant too much to him to be criticized by anyone. Especially her.

"I wish you'd have told me. He sounded like an amazing person."

"He was," Damon said in a raw whisper, wondering when he'd stop missing him.

"I-I made something for you."

It was only when Angela said those words that he noticed the covered dish on the table. His stomach clenched again, this time with fear.

"You made something for me?" he said, wanting to make sure. Hoping he'd heard wrong.

She nodded. "I've been practicing for weeks. I hope you like it."

He inwardly groaned. He'd swallow whatever she gave him, if that meant she would stay. He carefully sat down, resisting the primal urge to run and lifted up the cover.

And stared.

It couldn't be.

It was impossible.

Oats porridge with chopped pears. She'd made it for him. He didn't care if it didn't taste good he'd force down every bite.

But he didn't have to. It was creamy and thick with plump raisins, a little sweeter than he'd remembered it but just as delicious, with cinnamon and nutmeg transporting him back to his childhood. His heart swelled and he nearly wept with joy.

"I'm sorry," Angela said. "When you told me why you didn't want the surgery, I heard you but I didn't listen. I have a bad habit of doing that. It's because I hate feeling helpless. Growing up I learned to block any of my mother or sister's grievances so that I could ignore them and just get on with my day. With my life." Angela sighed. She didn't notice that Damon wasn't listening, that he was slowly savoring every bite. What she had to say held too much importance.

"I wanted things to be simple. If I could find a problem with a straightforward solution I grabbed it. That's what I did with you. I didn't want to think about what you would lose, how it would affect you because there was nothing I could do about it.

"But I get it now and I won't force you. I accept you as you are. You frustrate me at times, but that doesn't stop me from loving you."

He kept his voice and gaze low. "You love me?"

"Yes. But that means you have to accept me as much as I accept you. I will always fight for you. I've already done a ton of research about this disease and Vanessa's been helping me find out even more. There are experimental treatments, a lot less invasive surgery they're trying in Canada and other medications. I only want you to consider these options. That's all I ask."

Damon set the spoon down. A bottomless peace swept through him. She was offering him a choice, not an ultimatum. The future wouldn't be easy, but she wouldn't leave him. She accepted him—loved him—completely. "I will." He stood. His eyes met hers. "I will consider it all."

Angela rushed into his arms and he covered her mouth in a searing kiss that sealed his words as a vow. He reluctantly pulled away, took her hand and turned. "We have to go," he said in an urgent voice.

Angela stared at his back both breathless and confused. His kiss had left her senses spinning. "Go where?"

Damon glanced over his shoulder and gave her one of his rare, genuine smiles. One that lightened his eyes and filled her heart with happiness. It was s smile that promised her a future with him. "To Jadin," he said. "We have to go and bring him home."

ABOUT THE AUTHOR

Dara Girard, an award-winning, national bestselling author of more than forty novels, from romance to suspense, loves telling stories.

Born in the US to immigrant parents, Dara enjoys pulling from her Jamaican, British, Nigerian heritage and exposure to various cultures to bring what reviewers and fans call "vivid emotional stories" to life. She is best known for her popular Henson Series, the mysterious Clifton Sisters, and the fun Black Stockings Society.

You can write her at:
contactdara@daragirard.com
or
P.O. Box 10345
Silver Spring, MD 20914
If you'd like to receive a reply, please send a self-addressed stamped envelope.

Visit her website to sign up for her newsletter and get sneak peeks, monthly updates on new releases, and special offers.

For more information visit
www.daragirard.com

www.ingramcontent.com/pod-product-compliance
Lightning Source LLC
Chambersburg PA
CBHW021308190726
48288CB00003B/742